It is difficult to separate the story of
this fine novel from the story of the man
who wrote it, for "And A Threefold Cord"
is out of the author's life experience –
without being autobiographical. It is the
story of a district and an existence that
he knows well, of a people he loves, about
whom he writes with intimacy and care.
"And A Threefold Cord" deals with events
in the ghetto of a South African city, a
ghetto perched on the edge of Cape Town.
It is a district that pulsates with hate
and love, with the despair of poverty and
with the passion for freedom from apartheid. Here we follow the Pauls family in
their struggle to keep alive: Charlie and
his brothers Ronny and Jorny, his sister,
Caroline, his mother and his aging father.
With them we live the lesson they learn –
that survival lies in joining together . . .
It is a brave story, deeply moving, tense
in its unfolding. It is a story told by a
man who is loved for his courage and for
his integrity by his South African people.

SEVEN SEAS BOOKS

A Collection of Works by Writers in the English Language

ALEX LA GUMA

AND A THREEFOLD CORD

AND A
THREEFOLD
CORD

by

ALEX
LA GUMA

SEVEN SEAS PUBLISHERS
BERLIN

SEVEN SEAS BOOKS are published by
SEVEN SEAS PUBLISHERS BERLIN
Berlin W 8, Glinkastrasse 13–15

The names of all characters in
this book are fictitious

Published as a Seven Seas Book 1964
Copyright © 1964 by Alex La Guma
Cover Design by Lothar Reher
Printed by Graphische Werkstätten Berlin
License Number 306/122/64
Manufactured in the German Democratic Republic

This is for
Blanche
with love

Two are better than one; because they have a good reward for their labour.

For if they fall, the one will lift up his fellow: but woe to him that is alone when he falleth; for he hath not another to help him up.

Again, if two lie together, then they have heat, but how can one be warm alone?

And if one prevail against him, two shall withstand him; and a threefold cord is not quickly broken.

ECCLESIASTES IV: 9–12

Foreword

It is difficult to propound the cult of "art for art's sake" in South Africa. Life presents problems with an insistence which cannot be ignored, and there can be few countries in the world where the people, of all races and classes, are more deeply preoccupied with matters falling generally under the heading of "political". The doctrine of apartheid permeates every sphere of life, and whether you be member of Parliament, businessman, worker, priest, sportsman or artist you cannot escape its consequences. If art is to have any significance at all, it must reflect something of this national obsession, this passion which consumes and sometimes corrodes the soul of the South African people.

Some writers, caught in the cross-currents of fierce political controversy, appalled by the intensity of racial conflict, have, it is true, lapsed into a silence rather than commit themselves to the making of a judgment. But on the whole the young South African literature, more particularly that of the English-speaking writers, has shown an intense awareness of "the race question", and the most successful and profound literature has been produced by those who have loved life and truth well enough not to shrink from the facts. It is not easy for all South Africans, however well-intentioned, to know the facts. Divisions between Black and white are so sharp, points of contact so few, that real intimacy is rare, indeed in many cases punishable by law.

Whites writing about the lives of Blacks must often rely on intuition and guesswork rather than experience; this has led to superficiality of treatment and a falsification no less regrettable because unintentional.

The work of South Africa's Non-white writers has done a great deal to correct the perspective, though they themselves have found it no easier than their white colleagues to present a fully rounded picture of the South African scene. But the Non-white writer has possessed one great advantage, and that is detailed knowledge of the conditions and situations which contribute to the making of the South African tragedy. While the white, protected and cushioned by law, custom and the comparative ease of his life, observes the South African struggle from afar, somewhat in the position of a war correspondent describing the course of a conflict in which he is not directly involved, the Non-white writes as a participant on the field of battle itself. No Non-white, be he worker or peasant, doctor or lawyer, businessman or teacher, can escape the clutches of the apartheid monster. The African, no matter how high his station in life, is ever at the mercy of a policeman raiding for a pass. The Coloured youth is prevented by law and white trade union practice from acquiring training for skilled work. The Indian is expelled from his home under the Group Areas Act. It is in the lives of the Non-white people that the South African drama is played out with the greatest intensity. Their joy and sorrow, happiness and hardship are experienced with a depth of emotion which is quite beyond the range of experience of most whites. For this reason it is most likely that when the "South African Tragedy" comes to be written, its author will be a Non-white. To say this is not racialism but realism.

Of the younger writers in South Africa today, one of the most promising is Alex La Guma, a Coloured man born and bred in Cape Town, the most mature and multi-racial of all South African cities. Son of Jimmy La Guma, one of the outstanding leaders of the Non-white liberation movement and a member of the Central Committee of the Communist Party of South Africa, Alex has had politics in his life from the year of his birth, 1925, right up to the present day. As a young man he joined the Communist Party himself and was a member of the Cape Town District Committee of the Party until it was banned by the Nationalist Government in 1950. The succeeding years saw him no less active in the political sphere. He was one of those who took a foremost part in the preparations for the Congress of the People, the great mass gathering of representatives of all sections of the South African people which met at Kliptown, Johannesburg, in 1955, to draw up the historic declaration of rights known as the Freedom Charter. On December fifth of the following year, he was one of the 156 men and women of all races who were rounded up by the police all over the country and flown by military plane to Johannesburg to stand trial on a charge of treason – the Crown arguing that the demands for democratic rights set forth in the Freedom Charter were of so radical a nature that the organisers must have envisaged the overthrow of the Government by violence as the only means of bringing them about. It took nearly five years of legal argument and political struggle before the charges were thrown out by the court and the accused enabled to return to their normal lives.

Life for the political person and the rebel in South Africa, however, is never normal. The treason trial was not yet over before the country was plunged into further turmoil following the shooting of the anti-pass demonstrators at Sharpeville and Langa and the declaration of a state of emergency by the Nationalist Government in 1960. Ruling by decree, the Government arrested 20 000 people throughout the country. Some dubbed "idlers" and "tsotsis" were hastily processed through secret trials in the jails and shanghaied to forced labour in remote districts. Over 2000 of the top political leaders of the people were detained in prison without trial for periods up to five months. Among them was Alex La Guma, by this time an executive member of the Coloured People's Congress which, with the African National Congress, the Indian Congress and the White Congress of Democrats, was working for the implementation of the principles contained in the Freedom Charter. He spent the weary months of incarceration reading and writing, preparing himself for the career on which he was later to be launched with so much promise.

Alex has been a voracious reader all his life, and from an early age had tried his hand at writing. His first professional efforts, however, were probably as a member of the staff of the progressive newspaper *New Age,* whose staff he joined in 1956 and whose pages he illuminated with many striking vignettes of Coloured life and tragedy in Cape Town. He continued with the paper until August, 1962, when shortage of funds forced the reduction of staff to the bare minimum.

Meanwhile he had continued with his political work, and was no whit discouraged by the persecution to which he was subjected by the authorities.

In 1961, Nelson Mandela, spokesman of the National Action Committee appointed by the All-in African

Conference held in Maritzburg, called for the staging of a three-day strike at the end of May. The strike was in protest against the inauguration of the Verwoerd Republic, and in support of the demand for the calling of a national convention of all races. The demand further stipulated that a new democratic constitution for South Africa be drawn up. The Coloured People's Congress immediately pledged its full support. Alex La Guma and his colleagues threw themselves into the task of organising the people, but were arrested and detained without bail for twelve days under a new law passed by the Government specially to deal with the threat posed by the strike call. Although their leaders were in jail or in hiding during the crucial period before the strike was due to start, the Coloured people responded magnificently, and Cape Town industry and commerce suffered heavily during the three days of the strike.

Government repression had slowly convinced the people that non-violent struggle was failing to produce results; in December, 1961, a series of bomb explosions ushered in a new phase of struggle: the military wing of the underground African National Congress, *Umkhonto we Sizwe* (Spear of the Nation), directed its attacks against Government buildings and installations in various parts of the country. The Government's reply was the notorious Sabotage Act, passed during the following session of Parliament, and providing *inter alia* for the leading opponents of the Government to be placed under house arrest by decree of the Minister of Justice. In December, 1962, Alex La Guma was served with a notice confining him to his house for twenty-four hours a day. The only visitors permitted him for the five years duration of the notice were his mother, his parents-in-law and a doctor and lawyer who had not been named or banned. Another provision of the Sabotage Act was that nothing Alex La Guma said or wrote could be reproduced in any form in South Africa.

The immediate consequence of this was that Alex's first novel, *A Walk in the Night*, published in 1962 by Mbari Publications in Nigeria, became forbidden reading for all South Africans. A few copies were smuggled into the country and passed from hand to hand. The book won instant recognition as a work of talent and imagination.

It is a short novel – barely ninety pages long. But within its covers teem the variegated types of Cape Town's District Six. Alex La Guma knows and loves District Six and its people, and has written of them with intimacy and care. He has also had a number of short stories published in various magazines both in South Africa and abroad.

During his period of house arrest he worked on his second novel, *And A Threefold Cord*, this time dealing with life in one of the shanty-towns sprawled on the periphery of Cape Town.

Few white South Africans can have any conception of what life in a shanty-town is like, for here are housed the tens of thousands of Non-whites for whom there is no "official" place to live, Coloureds and Africans clutching precariously to life on the outskirts of the cities which offer their only hope of sustenance. Many of the inhabitants are in the urban area illegally, lacking the papers which establish their right to existence, a prey to perpetual police raids, insecurity and poverty. Home for them is a crazily-constructed shack providing only the barest shelte from the elements.

There are no paved streets, sanitation, drainage or

electric light in these areas; water has to be bought by the canful. In the Cape winter, when the rain comes pouring down, the roofs leak and the whole neighbourhood becomes sodden and waterlogged. Over all hovers the smell of dirt and wretchedness. Children play in the mud, and men and women flounder in the dark going to and from work – if they are lucky enough to have work. These are areas where life is short and cheap, where violence flares out of hate and frustration, yet where humanity, love and hope sprout even from the dunghill of evil and decay.

And a Threefold Cord is drenched in the wet and misery of the Cape winter, whose grey and dreary tones Alex La Guma has captured in a series of graphic prose-etchings. Under a lesser pen, it could have been depressing, this picture of South Africa's lower depths, with its incidents of sordid brutality and infinite desolation. But Alex La Guma's compassion and fidelity to life have infused it with a basic optimism. His electric dialogue crackles with the lightning of the human spirit. His message is: "People can't stand up to the world alone, they got to be together."

The fact that he was living under twenty-four-hour house arrest, and was thus completely cut off from all possibility of political action, did not save Alex La Guma from still further victimisation at the hands of the Government. Following the passing of the ninety-day no-trial Act by the South African Parliament in 1963, Alex La Guma was one of those who was arrested and detained without trial. In prison he was held in solitary confinement, locked in his cell alone for twenty-three and a half hours a day, the remaining half-hour being allowed for "exercise" – also on his own.

As was the case with other detainees, he was denied

15

visitors and any reading or writing material, refused access to his legal adviser and generally subjected to the most abominable form of mental torture so that he might be forced to answer questions to the satisfaction of the police. His wife Blanche, a nursing midwife, was also detained, and their two children had to be cared for by Mr. La Guma's mother. Blanche La Guma was later released, but almost immediately served with a banning order which prohibits her attendance at all gatherings, political or social, forbids her to communicate in any way with any other named or banned person, and restricts her to the Wynberg magisterial district in which she lives. In due course Alex himself was released – but on bail, facing a charge (at the time of writing) of being in possession of banned literature. If convicted, he may be sentenced to a term of imprisonment up to three years. Meanwhile he continues under twenty-four-hour house arrest, completely isolated from his fellow human beings.

It is to be hoped that the publication of *And A Threefold Cord* by Seven Seas Books will win for Alex La Guma the international reputation he deserves. It is hoped that this book will stimulate a world-wide campaign which will force the Verwoerd regime to restore to him and to all other political prisoners their full freedom. For no less than this is demanded in the resolution, passed by 106 votes to 1 (South Africa) by the United Nations General Assembly in October, 1963. It is time for effective action to be taken to end the nightmare of apartheid and repression in South Africa. It is time that men like Alex La Guma were able to come into their own, and live like free people in the land of their birth.

BRIAN BUNTING

Chapter One

In the north-west the rainheads piled up, first in cottony tufts blown by the high wind, then in skeins of dull cloud, and finally in high, climbing battlements, like a rough wall of mortar built across the horizon, so that the sun had no gleam, but a pale phosphorescence behind the veil of grey. The sea was grey, too, and metallic, moving in sluggish swells, like a blanket blown in a tired wind. The autumn had come early that year, and then the winter, and now the sky was heavy with the promise of rain. Along the coast, and in the parks in the cities, and in the country-side, the leaves had gone from the trees, and only on the slopes of the mountains and the peaks along the shoreline the pines and port-jackson and some oaks were dark-green in the greyness, and the earth bore a healthy dark-brown colour.

The first rain came in the form of a fine, blown mist, and it left a film of wetness on the earth and on the park benches and the steep, flat sides of buildings; and the asphalt of the streets and the roadways was black with it. Then the rain was gone, leaving only the dampness in the air, and the threat of more to come.

Then it was July and the laden clouds marched in from the ocean, commanded by the high wind, to limp, footsore, across the sky and against the ramparts of the mountains. For a while the mountains held them at bay, so that the rain harried only the coastline, and a veil of rain hung over the barbed peaks. The flanks of the rain fell into the sea. The high, grey-uniformed fog closed the mountains from the sky and the rest of the world, and hung like an omen over the land.

Some of the rain slipped through the breaches in the coastline and pelted inland to assault the suburbs, falling quickly and retreating again, so that there were trickles of moisture on windows in the morning, and dampness on the concrete of the long road pushing north, and a sheen on the wide-curving metal of railway lines. Beyond the city the earth received the rain and drank it, sucking down the moisture, and grew dark-brown and afterwards, black. The earth drank its fill from the intermittent falls, and when it was saturated, its surface was damp, so that when a man put down his foot the ground subsided under his weight and there were curved ridges moulded into the soil where he had walked, or if he had been barefooted, small hollows made by heel and ball of foot, and tiny hollows by his toes.

The people of the shanties and the *pondokkie* cabins along the national road and beside the railway tracks and in the suburban sand-lots watched the sky and looked towards the north-west where the clouds, pregnant with moisture, hung beyond the mountain. When the bursts of rain came, knocking on the roofs, working-men carried home loads of pilfered corrugated cardboard cartons, salvaged rusted sheets of iron and tin to reinforce the roofs. Heavy stones were heaved onto the lean-tos and patched roofs, to keep them down when the wind rose.

The children played in the puddles and the muddy soil, bare toes squishing into the wetness. And: Man, I struck a luck, man – got a tin of bitumen for five bob. Over the wall. Bitumen is all right for keeping out the water. Soak old sacking in it and stuff it into the cracks and joints. Reckon it's going to rain bad this year? I reckon so, man. Old woman is complaining about her rheumaticks awready, man. Say, give me my can of red on a cold day, and it can rain like a bogger, for all I care. Listen, chommy, I remember one time it rain one-and-twenty days in a row – non-stop. Arwie is going to bring home some tar. He works *mos* by the Council. Look there, I don't like that hole there. Johnny, you must fix it, instead of sitting around doing blerry nothing. Rain, rain, go away, come back another day, the children sang.

The sky was heavy and grey, shutting out the sun, and there was no daylight, but an unnatural, damp twilight. The rain began again with gusty bursts, showering the world, pausing and then pouring down in big heavy drops. Then it settled gradually into a steady fall, an unhesitant tempo of drops, always grey.

Chapter Two

The sound of water coming through the roof of the Pauls house awakened Charlie. The rain leaned against the house, under the pressure of the wind, hissing and rattling on the corrugated iron sides, scouring the roof. The wind flung the rain against the house with a roar, as if in anger, and then turned away, leaving only a steady hissing along the poorly painted, blistered metal.

Charlie Pauls turned in the sagging, loose sprung, iron bedstead, one arm curled up across his face and over his head, the other hand beneath, supporting the biceps. He heard the downpour outside through his sleep, and still sleeping, hauled the old army blanket up over his shoulders. Turning again, his arm swung outward from his face and the back of his hand struck something and he mumbled. Then, rising to the surface of sleep, he heard the sound of the water coming into the room, through the other sound of the rain against the sides of the house.

At first it was a hesitant drip-drip onto the plank floor; then a quicker, steadier plop-plop-plopping. Charlie opened his eyes, groaning, feeling the drool of saliva on his chin, wiping it away. Darkness enclosed him with the blackness of a sealed cave, and he lay in the darkness and listened to the tapping of the water that dropped from the ceiling.

There were smells in the room, too. The smell of sweat and slept-in blankets and airless bedding, close by; and somewhere indefinite, the smell of stale cooking and old dampness and wet metal. He did not take particular notice of these, but listened instead to the dripping of the water. In another part of the room, one of his brothers rolled and bounced and cursed in his sleep on another iron bedstead. He knew that was Ronald.

Charlie sat up and let the old army blanket fall over his raised knees. He slept in his underwear, almost impervious to the chill. He rubbed sleep out of his eyes and they gradually became accustomed to the dark, so that he could make out the shapes of things in the room: the muttering, tossing length of Ronald, the angular bulk of the wardrobe, and the other bed where Jorny slept.

Charlie reached out and groped with his left hand, found the apple-box which served as a bedside table, and searched its surface, past his tin of cigarettes and the coverless paperback, until he found the box of matches. He struck one in the dark, and peered around in the feeble, quivering light that blew in the draught which always came through the numerous crevices in the house; then peering hard into the half-light, found the puddle of water that was forming on the floor by the battered, cracked-mirrored, loose-hinged wardrobe. The match went out and he struck another, swinging his bare feet out onto the floor.

The planks were cold under his feet. He stood up, stooping under the low ceiling, and went over to the wall shelf, protecting the match flame with his cupped hand while he turned up the chimney of the storm-lantern, and lit the wick. When the wick was burning, he shook the match until the flame had died and dropped the burnt-out stick on the floor.

The wind rose again outside and drove the rain against the house, rumbling on the metal for a few moments, and then the wind turned away once more, on another tack, abandoning the low rattling and tapping.

Charlie turned up the wick in the storm-lantern, so that the flame swelled and brightened, throwing light around. Charlie's face, brown-skinned, glowed in the light which picked up the wide curves of his high cheek-bones and the thick, solid jaw running into a chin as curved and hard as the toe of an army boot. There was a dark stubble in the hollows of his cheeks, and deep grooves bracketed the wide, heavy, humorous and sensual mouth. He had a wide forehead, and low, with the dark, thick, kinky hair growing far forward. There was a mole on his right cheekbone. His eyes were dark-brown, the colour of chestnuts, gleaming in the lamp-light, the eyeballs yellowish.

He left the lamp and searched around in the narrow, box-like room until he found the dented four-gallon paraffin can, and carried it over to where the leakage in the ceiling was making the pool on the floor of the room. On his way there, the can bumped the iron bed-stead on which Ronald slept, and the slam of the tin woke him.

Ronald woke up with a jerk, sitting upright in the bed against the cardboard partition wall that separated them from the kitchen, with a sudden startled movement, while he said loudly: "Hey. Hey. What –"

Charlie placed the can on the floor under the drip from the ceiling. The plop-plopping sound was turned suddenly into a tiny rumbling as the drops struck the metal, and then gradually became a dull tinkling.

Charlie said, going back to his bed: "Sorry I made

you awake, man. Blerry rain coming in." Under his heavy body the worn, gritty floor moved, sagging.

He sat on the bed in his soiled underwear. The other brother, Jorny, slept with his face to the wall, under an old, disembowelled quilt, his dark, cropped head alone showing. The rain hissed on against the house.

Ronald remained sitting up in the bed, rubbing his eyes. Charlie reached for his cigarette tin, opened it, and lighted a cigarette. The tiny window between their two beds shook under the driving wind and rain.

"You been dreaming?" Charlie asked, blowing smoke through his nostrils and looking across at Ronald. He smiled, revealing his strong, big, yellowish teeth. "Man, you was going on as if you had that Susie Meyer in that bed with you, *mos*. Jumping and pushing."

"What? Whatter?" Ronald asked, flushing and staring at his elder brother. "Who said I was dreaming? What the hell you got to do with me?"

Charlie grinned. "Not *you*, man. Susie Meyer."

"Then what you got to do with Susie?" Ronald asked, belligerently. He was also somewhat embarrassed, and scowled at Charlie.

"Why the hell don't you marry the goose and you don't have to dream, man?" Charlie asked. He was beginning to enjoy the provocation of Ronald.

Ronald said loudly: "Listen here, hey. You listen here, *jong*. Leave me alone, hey."

Charlie said, through the cigarette smoke: "You'll make the lighty awake." He motioned with a thumb towards where Jorny was sleeping.

"Well, how come you don't leave me alone then?" Ronald whined. "Always picking, picking."

"Gwan, man," Charlie said, and slid back under his blanket, but resting on one elbow so he could continue

23

smoking. "Man just making sports with you. You don't need to get on your little horse every time a man mention that Susie Meyer." And he chuckled.

Ronald glowered at him, waiting for his brother to say something else. The wind had dropped and there was only the sound of the rain and the plunking of the leak. Charlie looked up at the spot through which the water was dripping and murmured: "Better fix that place up in the morning."

Ronald relaxed, still looking sullen, and sank into the hollow of his mattress, staring watchfully at Charlie over the edge of his blanket.

"Wind gone down," Charlie remarked. The boy, Jorny, muttered in his sleep and wriggled under the tattered quilt. Charlie looked across and up at the cheap tin alarm-clock on the shelf in another part of the room. "Almost time to get up." He turned his eyes towards the window. It was just a square porthole cut in the wall and fitted with a pane of dusty glass. Outside, beyond the veil of water, the world was black and wet. The flame in the storm-lamp and the oily smoke warmed the air slightly, so Charlie decided not to put it out. He finished his cigarette and crushed the butt on the floor beside his bed.

He yawned loudly, and then said with pretended seriousness: "She got a blerry nice pair of poles, though."

Ronald had been waiting for such a remark. He howled and reached down for one of his shoes and flung it. It sailed across the room, just missing the lantern and Charlie, waiting for it, raised an arm casually, stopping the shoe in mid air and it fell with a thump onto the floor.

Ronald was sitting up in bed again, his eyes wide and

his face working as he glared at Charlie. He shouted, almost in tears, "You better stop it, hey. I'm telling you, you better stop it."

Charlie scowled, saying, "Cut it out, man. You almost set the blerry place alight."

"Well, you better blerry well stop it," Ronald shouted.

In another part of the house, bed springs creaked and sang like a broken harp, and their mother's voice cried, "Whatter goes on in there with you boys? Get up or go to sleep, but let your pa get his rest."

"Okay, Ma, okay," Charlie called out. "The rain is coming inside and I had to put a *blik*, a tin, down." He was sitting on the edge of the bed again.

"Your pa want to rest," Ronald said with a small sneer. "Your pa got to have his rest. The *ou* rest all bladdy day."

Charlie reached across to where his jeans hung over the bar of the foot of the bedstead and dragged it towards him. He said, "You leave the *ou kerel* alone. You got no right raising that sort of voice about the old man." He worked his legs into the jeans and then stood up, jerking it around his waist.

Ronald said, "Huh."

Charlie buttoned the jeans and then buckled the worn, scarred army belt, wrenching the strap to lock the spike of the brass buckle through the hole. He said, again, while he did this, "You got no right to talk about Dad that way." He sat down on the bed again and stooped to find his boots. "You just stick to *ou* Susie Meyer."

"There, you starting again, hey," Ronald said.

"Okay, forget it, man," Charlie grinned. "Forget it. Man can't make a joke with you." He pulled on his boots and stamped to get them well on, then he crossed his legs to lace them. "Look like the rain held up a little," he said. He looked at the window. The glass was still running with broken raindrops, but the dark behind it had taken on a greyness.

Charlie said, "It's funny, *ne*, I got no work but I'm first up in the morning, and you's always blerry last. Bet you clock in on the tippy."

Ronald said, "I'm not putting me out for that blerry old job."

"They'll give you the sack, man."

"Well, I'm not married to the job, *mos*."

Charlie opened his mouth to say something about marriage and Susie Meyer, but he changed his mind and laughed instead, saying, "You reckon."

The boy, Jorny, woke up and looked with sleep thickened eyes across the quilt at them. "*Howkees*," he whined. "You *ouens* make a lot of noise."

Ronald snapped, threateningly, at him, "Hey, lighty –"

"Sleep some more, *pikkie*," Charlie cut in. "It's still early."

He lit another cigarette from his tin and then got up and walked towards the room door. The rain had stopped hissing now, and had assumed a faint tapping against the corrugated iron sides of the house.

Charlie was tall and had the big shoulders and chest of one who had worked with his muscles. The muscles bunched and knotted under the long-sleeved, soiled flannel vest. His shadow reared against the wall over Ronald's bed, like a black phantom thrown by the light. He moved over to the door in his worn boots, the cigarette dangling from a corner of his wide, mobile mouth, the smoke drifting up past the cheekbone, so that one eye screwed up to avoid the fumes.

He turned his head to gaze at the ceiling. The flattened cartons and sheets of composition board which made up the ceiling were stained and warped and discoloured from past winters, and where the new leak had started during the night, a spreading black map of dampness had started. The drip of water had slowed down to a reluctant rapping into the tin below it.

"It's that end where the zinc got loose," Charlie said to himself, looking at the spot. "Hope the rain hold up so I can fix it." He removed the cigarette from his mouth and flicked ash into the can on the floor. There was about two inches of water in the bottom of the can.

Ronald said, sitting on his bed, "Dammit. Now a man's got to go to work in the blerry rain." He had commenced dressing, and he was chilled and surly.

Chapter Three

Charlie opened the door and went out into the dark kitchen. He struck a match and found another storm-lamp. It hung from a beam across the bulging cardboard ceiling. When he had lighted the lamp it picked out spots of shining points in the kitchen: the row of battered, black-bottomed saucepans hanging above the old iron stove, the blade of the butcher-knife dangling against the side of the dresser from a loop of dirty string through a hole in the end of its handle, the metal top of the cracked sugar bowl on the dresser shelf.

The kitchen floor sagged and groaned under Charlie's weight. The rain tapped at the kitchen door, like somebody trying to get in. Another room led off the kitchen, and from beyond the thin, washed-out curtain over its doorless entrance came the sounds of movement, the creaking of a bed, the thump of a shoe kicked across the floor.

Then his mother's voice called out, "That you, Charles? Put on the fire, old son."

From the same room came the wet, phlegm-laden cough-cough of an old man.

"Right, Ma," Charlie called back.

He went to the kitchen door and drew back the bolt and pulled the door open. A gust of wind and a shower of fine rain struck him, and he stepped back from the threshold, shivering with the sudden wet coldness. The rain fell on the doorstep and a little way into the kitchen. It was no longer a hard, sheeting rain, but small, sharp, scattered drops. Charlie held the cigarette end cupped in his hand and looked out through the doorway. The first biting chill had disappeared from his body, for it adapted itself quickly to the change of temperature. Still, there was goose-flesh on his chest.

The sky was a weighing black, but towards the east, far beyond the dark shapes of shacks and trees, it was turning a dish-water grey, just a smudged line above the distant, invisible mountains. And as if to endorse the coming of dawn, a rooster, somewhere among the shanties, crowed a strident reveille. The world dribbled and gurgled in the darkness. Another cock crowed, and then yet another, and a dog raised its voice in a high yap-yapping.

Charlie spun his cigarette butt out into the drizzle, watching the glowing tip go out swiftly in mid air and disappear. He shut the door, struck another match and dropped it through the hole in the top of the iron stove. The flame caught the papers under the wood-chips and the carefully placed scraps of coal, and the stove purred for a moment and then broke into a small roar. Charlie moved the enameled saucepan of water, waiting on one side of the stove, over the hole. Then he went back to his room.

In the brothers' room Ronald had finished dressing. He wore tight trousers, an old sweater with a stag design on the front of it, and a limp leather jacket. He was brushing his hair in front of the cracked, fly-blown mirror of the wardrobe. Neither of them had washed.

"Still raining?" he asked, putting the brush away on a shelf made of a tomato-box nailed to an upright of the wall. There was a small, dusty jar of thick, green pomade on the shelf, besides the brush, and the skeleton of a plastic comb, dry entrails of hair clinging stubbornly to its broken ribs.

"*Ja*," Charlie said, and sat down on his bed. One could not stand very long in a stooped position in the room. "But not so much. Just a little. It will hold up later, I think."

"How you know it's going to hold up?" Ronald asked, with a little scorn in his voice. "How you know such a lot about when the rain will stop and how long it'll go on? You's *mos* clever, man. Don't I say?"

"Hell, I don't know a lot about it," Charlie told him, sitting with his elbows on his knees in the sagging room, and his big wide hands dangling between his legs. "Who said I know a lot? I'm just thinking so, man." He grinned at Ronald. "Awright, wise guy. What you so worried about things? Worried about rain, worried about that Susie Meyer."

Ronald jerked a look at him, shining his shoes with a balding brush, placing first one foot on a ledge of wood and then another. "Who said I'm worried over Susie Meyer? You starting again, hey?"

Charlie laughed. "Awright, but those shoes is going to look like crack once you start running for the bus." Ronald was a bit of a dandy.

"Okay, that's *mos* my business, don't I say?" Ronald said. He put the shoe brush on top of the wardrobe and went out to the kitchen.

"Food ready?" Charlie heard him ask, gruffly.

Then the mother's voice replied. "Wait a little. I would say morning first."

"Morning, then," Ronald grumbled. "How, man, must a man always wait for his diet?"

"What you so troublesome for?" the mother asked, sharply. "You getting too big for your boots."

Charlie chuckled to himself. Then he got up and went to the wardrobe, opened the limp door, and pulled out his old khaki shirt from a bundle inside. He flopped the shirt open, and pulled it on over his head. He walked to the kitchen again, thrusting the tails into the top of his faded jeans.

Chapter Four

Ronald was sitting on the bench against the wall behind the scrubbed deal table, wolfing down the hot, cooked oats from a chipped enamel plate before him. The kitchen, like the rest of the house, was small and cramped, and everybody moved cautiously in it, retreating and advancing with care to avoid collisions. The bench and a few boxes, all of which could be stored under the table, took the place of chairs, and the walls were hung with blackened utensils. The walls were of old corrugated iron, patchily painted inside, held upright by salvaged wooden supports. An old calendar with a picture of a fly-spotted boy with curly blonde hair and blue eyes, fondling a mongrel pup with a happy face, hung behind the kitchen door. The title of the picture was "Chums", but the word had been obliterated by a brown stain, along with the name of the furniture store which had issued the calendar. The cardboard ceiling bulged and the menfolk walked with a stoop under it, and it was dark and mouldy with dampness. There was a musty smell in the house, which nobody really bothered about.

Ronald crouched morosely at the table, gulping down his breakfast. The lamplight glowed on the pomade on his hair. Adolescence lay heavily on him, reflected in his mean brown eyes, in the twist of his bitter mouth, and a reckless truculence scratched at the hard enclosure of his mind, vicious as a watchdog at a gate.

Charlie said, coming into the warmth of the kitchen, with its smell of smoking wood and boiling oats, "Morning, Ma. The blerry roof is leaking again."

"You got to do something about it," the mother said, speaking from where she stood at the stove. "Is damp in our room, too." And to Ronald: "You better make quick. You'll miss that first bus." Then back to Charlie, "The whole house look like it's falling in. I don't know what to do with your pa sick."

"Sick," Ronald said, scraping the last of the porridge in his plate and getting up at the same time. "That *ou* been sick a helluva time."

"You stop talking about your pa like that," the mother said, sharply.

Charlie looked at his younger brother. "You got nothing to say, hey. Helluva lot *you* do around this blerry place."

"Picking," Ronald shouted back, gathering up the parcel of thick sandwiches at the side of his plate. "Always picking, picking, picking."

"Keep quiet, *bliksem*," Ma Pauls threatened, holding a ladle like a weapon. "Keep quiet and go to work."

Ronald jammed the sandwiches under the leather jacket and went towards the door, bumping the table aside. He stood scowling with his back towards them, wrenching at the bolt until he had the door open. The thin rain swept in like a blown curtain of liquid lace, splattering him.

He said, "You just keep on picking." Then he was gone into the paling darkness, slamming the door behind him.

"I don't know what's going to happen with him," Ma said, wiping a strand of hair from her face and leaving a smear of oats on her forehead. "*Him*, and your pa so sick, and Ca'line going to have her child anytime now. Don't a person have enough troubles to think about?"

"*Ach,* Ronny's awright," Charlie said. "He will still come right, *you* see, Ma." He grinned at the old woman. "Well, I'll go see how the old toppy is this morning."

He left the mother and went behind the curtain into the other room. A candle burned, trembling in the draught, on a limp chest of drawers which stood lop-sidedly on the uneven floor, making a half-glow on the ramshackle room. In the big, sagging, rattling iron bed, Dad Pauls peered out from a jumble of old bedding. The candlelight picked out the whites of his eyes and gleamed on a brass knob at the head of the bedstead.

Once, long ago, Dad Pauls had been a strong, tall man, but now he was a framework of bones, a child's drawing of a man, his dark face clawed by want and sickness, hollow and ravaged, the stark bones showing under the thin skin, an outlandish mask hurriedly and roughly cut out of brown, seamed wood. His bony knees, drawn up under the bedding, made tall peaks that quivered like a miniature earthquake; the whole body shivered and shook in the bed, gripped by sickness and the draught that came through crevices and old nail-holes in the walls of the room. His lipless mouth was open, and his emaciated, old chest wheezed and whispered like a tea kettle, the body-frame shaking like a mechanical toy.

Charlie stood at the foot of the bed and said quietly: "How you, Dad?"

The hollow eyes turned towards him and the mouth moved soundlessly, like that of a stranded fish. A sick old man clinging with brittle nails to the tortuous cliff of life, holding on with a last, desperate effort.

Charlie said, "Just res', Dad. You just res'." He

winked at the old man lying there, and went out again.

"Old boy look bad," he said when he came into the kitchen again. He sat down at the table, his big body hunched into the confined space. "How long this rain going to go on, you reckon, Ma?"

"Sometimes it is an eight-day rain," Ma said. "Look like a bad winter. It won't be good for your pa. I hope he can eat a little porridge this morning. Can't eat hardly nothing, poor man." She sighed. "There's people going to be washed out, when it begin. The rain. You better look at the *dingus,* the roof." She laid a plateful of steaming porridge before him.

"I'll take a look," Charlie said, starting to eat. He blew steam from his spoon. "Maybe it isn't so bad."

"And I wish that Ronny will behave himself. Wild as a horse, is he. Always shouting and grumbling and rude. He'll *op*set the old man, too, and make things worser."

"He'll be awright."

"He'll get into trouble. You will see, then we have to get him out again."

"Ah, he's only a lighty. He got a girl, *mos*, now. That Susie Meyer."

"*Ja,*" the mother said, stirring the remainder of the breakfast in the saucepan. "I heard stories about her. Missus Appolis was telling me she had a child by a married man, *mos*. And she go around with all kind of men. I don't like her, man. I hope Ronny don't get mix up with her."

"Ah, maybe she isn't so bad, Ma," Charlie said, sprinkling more sugar over his porridge. "Lot of girls have babies."

"Goddamit," Ma Pauls said. "Everybody's awright by you. Isn't so bad. Is awright. Everything is going to be okay. *You* not bringing up no children yet." She wiped her hands on a grey dish-rag. "And don't use up all the sugar. It must last till Friday."

Charlie grinned at her over his dripping spoon. "Awright, Ma. Awright, man. Don't go on so."

The rain hissed and clattered around the house. Outside, towards the east, the sky was still paling slowly with a bloodless light, going grey with caution, as if the morning was sneaking carefully past the sentries of drizzle.

In the sick-room the bed rattled and shook, and a moaning came from behind the curtain. Charlie said, scraping his plate clean with the edge of his spoon: "Old toppy is really bad."

"I'll take him some porridge just now," Ma said. "He ought to have lot of soup, I reckon." She went to the iron stove and found the chipped enamel coffee-kettle and carried it over to the table. Charlie watched while she poured coffee into a cup. The fine rain sounded against the sides of the house and drip-drip-dripped from the corners outside. In the boys' room the leak muttered liquidly into the tin can below it.

"Sound like it'll stop," Charlie said. He reached for the sugar.

"One spoon only," Ma told him. "I hope so. You got to fix up that roof before it get too bad."

Sitting hunched on the wooden box at the table, Charlie stirred his coffee, lifted the cup slowly and blew the steam away, sipped gingerly and blew steam away again, and then put the cup down gently in the cracked saucer. Ma Pauls was sitting on a bench by the stove, her head back against the wall, her eyes closed, as if she was dreaming of something. Charlie picked up his cup again, and drinking, listened to the rain outside. He could hear only the harsh, far-away swishing of trees like the rustle of paper teasers.

He put his cup down and went to the door and opened it. The rushing sound of the trees deepened with the door open, and the wind came in, cold, driving the drip from the eaves over the doorway into the kitchen, across the floor and blowing at the lamp, making the shadows jig across the smoky walls.

Ma Pauls opened her eyes in the rush of cold air and asked, "What's the matter? What is it?"

"Rain held up, I think," Charlie said.

"Close the door," Ma said.

Beyond the dark and muddy yard with the faint lamplight winking on the puddles in front of the kitchen door, beyond the heavy portjackson trees and the cowering jumble of shanties that huddled across the flats, the sky now held a whitish tinge, spreading gradually like a slow leak in the rim of the universe. The rain had stopped, but there was still the feel of it, like a menace, in the air.

Roosters were crowing among the shacks, and the brown shepherd mongrel whose name was "Watchman" loped out of the dwindling darkness, his coat alight with moisture, and entered the kitchen.

"Get that dog out, and close the door," Ma scolded. "He'll mess up the blerry place."

"Out, Watchman, out," Charlie said, slapping at the dog, and then shut the door on it. "I wish it would hurry up and get light," he went on. "I want to get on the roof before it begin to rain again." The dog had left muddy paw-marks on the splintery floor.

Charlie went back to his room, sliding round the door that did not open all the way because of the wardrobe. The boy, Jorny, peeped at him over the edge of the thin quilt under which he lay on the camp stretcher. There was a yellow Corporation slicker hanging behind the door, and Charlie took it down, thrust his arms into the sleeves, jerking on the coat. He pulled on his ruined cloth cap. The leak in the ceiling had subsided to a reluctant dripping, but there was a big wet patch on the ceiling.

Charlie looked up at the stain, frowning, and then, big and bulky in the yellow slicker, he went out of the room.

Chapter Five

Dad Pauls had built the house a long time ago, when he and Ma had drifted from the country-side to the city. Ma had been pregnant with Caroline, and Ronald had been a dirty-nosed youngster hanging onto her skirts, whining like a hurt pup. Dad had rented the lot, one of the several empty ones in the sand waste just beginning to be crowded in by the collection of dilapidated shanties that was springing up like sores on the leg of land off the highway.

Some folks like themselves had taken Ma and Ronald in, while Dad and Charlie had camped under a stretch of blankets, to guard the family belongings and to work on the house. Frederick Pauls had worked desperately, so that he could have the shack built before Ma's time came, and before the bad weather set in. But he and Charlie had not made it, so Caroline had been born in a sort of chicken-run which was the only place where the people who had taken them in had been able to accommodate them.

Dad and Charlie had scavenged, begged and, on dark nights, stolen the materials for the house. They had dragged for miles sheets of rusty corrugated iron, planks, pieces of cardboard, and all the astonishing miscellany that had gone into building the house. There were flattened fuel cans advertising a brand of oil on its sides, tins of rusty nails which Charlie had pulled from the gathered flotsam and jetsam and straightened with a hammer on a stone; rags for stuffing cracks and holes, strips of baling wire and waterproof paper, cartons, old pieces of metal and strands of wire, sides of packing-cases, and a pair of railway sleepers.

Their best find had been the stove. It had been abandoned on a rubble heap, its sides cracked, two of the lids, the oven door and the smoke stack missing, and the whole covered with rust. Dad and Charlie had lifted it onto a crude sled and dragged it four miles down the road to their lot. Charlie had rubbed and scraped the rust off the stove and Dad had made a new smoke stack from sheets of tin and a couple of canisters. A man from one of the other cabins, who had edged his way into helping, had found a pair of broken fire-bricks.

Dad and Charlie, and now and then the other help, Coloured and African shack dwellers, had filled four-gallon cans with crudely-made concrete and allowed it to set. Then they had arranged the concrete-filled containers in a square and had laid the floor of the kitchen and the bedroom across them. Some of the flooring had been too short and had been joined clincher-wise, so that one tripped over the ridges if one did not know where they were located. Then the walls had gone up, an assortment of rusty galvanised sheets and flattened oil drums nailed and bound to uprights, with a square hole left in the bedroom for a window. Dad had pleaded the kitchen door from a demolition company, and had even managed to get the frame of the bedroom doorway with it, together with a few odd laths.

When the kitchen had been completed, they moved into it, together with the stove which was mounted on a platform of bricks. And living in the kitchen, they had gone ahead with the other room.

The winter set in and the foundations of concrete

cubes had sunk unevenly into the wet sand, so that the house began to sag crookedly and to take on a lopsided look. And when the bedroom was done, it appeared even crazier, as if the two sections would split off from each other at any moment. But Dad Pauls had hammered and nailed and lashed with wire, praying at the same time that the entire contraption would hold together.

The roof had been nailed down and they had heaved heavy stones on to it for additional security. In the end, Dad had even fashioned a little porch roof over the kitchen door, which was the only outer door of the house, and a railway sleeper had gone to make a step. Finally, the house had held out, warping here and cracking there, groaning like a prisoner on the rack, then settling down in the face of the seasons with the stubbornness of ancient ruins.

When Ronald and Charlie had grown older and the shack had become too cramped, they had built another room onto the kitchen, so that now the whole place had the precarious, delicately balanced appearance of a house of cards. The kitchen porch had gradually disappeared.

Now, stepping out of the house, Charlie, big in the yellow slicker, felt the mud of the yard squelch and gulp under his boots. The air was thick with a wet mist, but the drizzle had ceased.

He turned his head and called into the kitchen, "She's held up, Ma."

Overhead the sky was lightening steadily, and around him objects appeared, emerging from the thinning darkness: the stunted mulberry tree and the ribs of the sagging yard fence, the sheen of water in the pig puddle in the hollow of the yard, the glisten of moisture on the mud. Beyond and among the wet portjackson trees, other shanties crouched in the sucking quagmire of rain-blackened sand, and here and there a light burned like ghosts in a churchyard. A dog yap-yapped, and then a harsh choir created a crescendo against the gathering daylight.

Charlie walked around the house, his weight sinking into the mud, and he left behind him a soggy trail, quickly filled by brown water, around the wet, leaning, tin-and-lath side of the house, to where it faced the straggling, swampy lane between the ragged rows of tatterdemalion shacks, some of them crowded together as if to suck warmth from each other's dugs, others standing aloof with a sort of decrepit pride in their individual bogs.

There were people moving through the mud now, plodding and stumbling through the stickiness, bent under the grey threat of rain, towards the suburban road where the buses waited to carry them off towards the city or the blank industrial areas.

A man and a girl lurched past the Pauls house, trying to avoid the puddles in the hollow street. The girl wore rubber Wellington boots, shiny with wetness.

The man hailed Charlie, waving a spongy lunch parcel: "*Het,* Charlie, man. Dreary weather, hey?"

"*Ja,*" Charlie called over the tangled fence. "Still going to fall like a bogger, I think."

"Morning, Charlie," the girl called from under a strip of headcloth. She was wrapped in an old woollen coat that was already going sodden from the morning mist.

"Hullo, Margie."

They went up the churned street, and Charlie turned to the back of the house. The roof was low enough for him to reach up and feel its edge. At his feet one of the concrete blocks on which the edge of the floor had rested had sunk into the soft ground, leaving a gap between it and the house. Charlie went around the house again, back to the yard to where an old trestle lay by the empty chicken-run.

The shack across the yard was a big motor-car crate resting a few inches off the ground on pieces of timber. Charlie and Caroline's husband, Alfred, had brought it home on old Jannie Isaacs' wagon all the way from town where they had bought it. They'd knocked out a few planks to make a doorway, and used the same planks for the door. It did not fit very well and old sacks kept the draught out at night. They had nailed builder's waterproofing to the top which was the roof. Charlie had found some paint, too, and Alfred had done the painting. But there had not been enough to cover the whole cabin, so part of the word *Detroit* emerged where the paint ended.

Now Charlie carried the trestle to where he meant to climb onto the roof of the Pauls house. He placed the trestle by the side of the house and raised one foot onto the cross-bar, pressing down with his weight to test its strength. Then, satisfied that it would hold, heaved himself up, and his hands on the edge of the roof, swung swiftly up onto the top of the house, moving quickly in the yellow slicker before his weight could have any effect on the weakness of the shack.

But he felt the side of the house sag under him, and he thought, desperately, Oh, God, the whole effing thing is going to come down.

But it held, creaking soggily under him, and he moved with caution. Crouched in the yellow slicker, under the grey-flannel sky sagging with moisture, Charlie saw the rust-rotted ruin of the roof, the metal flaking and splintering away, and one long seam sprung loose. He crawled across, feeling with horror the scrap metal giving under his weight, and thought, Need a whole new piece of iron, dammit.

He clambered from the roof, feeling the place shake and quiver as if with a fever, and dropped into the bursting mud of the yard. Ma came around an angle of the shack.

Charlie said, "I'm going down to *ou* Mostert and see is he got some stuff we can use for the roof."

He considered the matter of the roof a serious proposition. Standing by the rusty wall, he felt the sharp wind blow in and rustle the yellow Corporation slicker he wore, and he hoped the rain would hold off.

Chapter Six

It could hardly be called a street, not even a lane; just a hollowed track that stumbled and sprawled between and around and through the patchwork of shacks, cabins, huts and wickiups: a maze of cracks between the jigsaw pieces of the settlement, a writhing battlefield of mud and straggling entanglements of wet and rusty barbed wire, sagging sheets of tin, toppling pickets, twigs and pealed branches and collapsing odds and ends with edges and points as dangerous as sharks' teeth, which made up the fencework around the quagmires of lots.

Along one side of the settlement, separating it like a fortification from where the houses of the suburb proper began, a rubbish dump lay like the back of a decaying monster, its scales of rotting paper, wood, offal, tin cans and indescribable filth, heaving and twitching in the stiff, damp breeze. Overhead the sky looked on with its sand-grey expression.

Making his way through the soggy labyrinth, Charlie watched the sky furtively, like a fox suspecting a trap. Now and then he raised a hand in salute to somebody behind a fence. There was life stirring in the wreckage around him: the punkpunk of an axe striking sodden wood, a scolding voice raised against a recalcitrant child. Scraps of washing hung out desperately, like tawdry bunting left over from a long-past celebration; a deputation of mongrels sniffing at some mysterious attraction behind a shack. Over everything hung the massed smell of pulpy mould, rotten sacking, rain, cookery, chickens and the rickety latrines that leaned crazily in pools of horrid liquid, like drunken men in their own regurgitation.

And then, coming around a corner of a loosely-strung wire fence, into a sort of square scarred and criss-crossed with rain-filled ruts and strewn with bits of dirty paper, Charlie heard his name spoken, and he looked aside and saw the little group by the ruined horse trough.

Changing his direction, he sauntered casually towards the gathering by the trough, and noticed that their conversation dwindled away into silence at his approach, like water from a leaking bucket. Curiosity and suspicion stirred him with a nagging touch, but he smiled, nevertheless, showing his square, yellow teeth through the stubble around his mouth.

There were five of them, a motley collection of scare-crows, dummies stuffed with the straw of poverty, clad in the unmatching tatters of jackets, trousers and head-gear, two of them barefooted, their hard, muddy feet seeking warmth in the doughy soil, their faces ageless, burnt-out and dark as charred wood.

Charlie said, "*Hoit,* men. I heard my name said."

Four cautious grins were turned towards the fifth in the group. He stood with two of the others behind the broken trough, and he wore no coat despite the chill of the air, while he frowned with bright eyes at Charlie Pauls.

"I was not talking about you, *ou* Charlie," this man said.

His damp blue shirt clung to his muscular shoulders, and he was thick with bone and flesh, but his belly was

46

round, sagging a little over his belt, and liquor had eroded him.

"That's awright," Charlie said. "I was just asking, *mos*." He rubbed the stubble on his chin with a hand. "You boys keeping awright?"

"Of course, *ja*, Charlie, of course, *ja*," the murmur came quietly from the four. They looked a little embarrassed and shifted on their feet, and kept looking at the thick man.

"Well, if you reckon you *must* know," this man said with sudden boldness and a small sneer in his voice, "we was talking about your other brother. That lighty, Ronny."

A small chorus of protest came up from the others. "Hey, *ou* Roman, no man. We didn't say nothing, hey. I say, *ou* Roman, let go, man. We *mos* did not say nothing man." And they shuffled in the mud, moving away from Roman as if absolving themselves from guilt, leaving him standing apart beyond the trough.

"What does it need then, man?" Charlie asked looking from face to face. "What's the matter, hey?" And to Roman: "What about Ronny?"

"Awright," Roman said. "You's *mos* his brother. I was just reckoning to these *jubas* I don't like that Ronny must worry with my goose. See?"

"What goose?" Charlie asked. "And you can *mos* tell Ronny that yourself. Don't I say?"

"Okay. But maybe you can *mos* take the message. Tell him to keep away from *ou* Susie." Roman stared with a mixture of aggression and disdain at Charlie.

Charlie shook his head and grinned. "Ach, . . . Worrying about a goose. Hell, man."

A black hound loped up, sniffed around the trough, urinated against its broken side, and moved off. Charlie watched it go. He heard Roman say, "I'm just warning you."

Standing bulkily in the yellow slicker, he looked again at Roman. He said: "Hey, man. Now you talking *strong,* mate. Warning. What you talking about warning? What warning?"

"Susie is *my* goose," Roman said. He had a heavy, rough-skinned face, like worn sandstone. "I'm only warning you, that lighty going to get into trouble."

"Listen," Charlie said, feeling irritable. "I don't take no warning for nobody. But let me give you a warning, man. You just leave *ou* Ronny alone. Awright?" He spoke calmly, and he was thinking, This *juba* want a fight, and if he start something I got to have a chance to get this oilskin off.

Roman looked dangerous, and said, "Now who's talking strong? You reckon I get a fright for you?"

"Ah, go and . . .," Charlie said, deciding to call it off. He started to turn away, but Roman came around the trough, crying: "No, wait a little, man. Don't blow, hey."

Charlie waited, his back half turned towards Roman, looking at the thick man over the yellow-slickered angle of his shoulder. The rest of the group slithered and shuffled in the mud, watching with the sharp, bright, alert eyes of crows. Everybody felt that Roman had to fight. It was like a mongrel snarling over a bitch against a rival.

Roman said, provocatively, "Don't run away now, pally. Don't run away."

Charlie said, turning towards him: "Who's running, man? What do you talk?"

"You *mos* talked strong." Roman was conscious of the eyes on him. Faces peered over gates and fences of some of the shacks around the muddy square, sniffing at the spectacle of trouble like dogs around a dustbin.

"And what about it?" asked Charlie. "Can't a man talk strong?"

"You and your brother," Roman sneered, pushing the matter. He did not want to let this drift from its original principle. "You *mos* reckon you can just take a *juba's* girl off."

"You talking crack," Charlie told him. "God, man, she's not your blerry wife. You got *mos* a wife. But go and see Ronny about that blerry goose. Not me."

"Now you talking about my wife, hey?" Roman said, shrilly, "You watch your mouth, you bastard."

Like an aggressive power waiting for an excuse to start a war, Roman now made up his mind to bring the talking to a conclusion, and he came up on Charlie, his shoulders hunched and his arms hooked, fists balled in front of his chest. "I'll *eff* you up, pally, and then it will be your brother afterwards."

Charlie said, "You just leave that lighty alone, understand. And further, don't talk so big about effing up." He backed off, watching Roman, while he unfastened the hooks that held together the front of the slicker.

The men around them cried, merrily, "There's water," and from across the square a woman's voice piped, "Hey, are you mad to fight. Just like blerry *skollies*, hooligans."

Charlie tossed the slicker over to one of the onlookers.

Roman waited no longer, but came in, in a squatting lunge, his left fist feinting, his right launching out. Charlie moved up, taking the right-armed blow on his elbow and threw it aside. Shifting his hips to avoid Roman ramming him in the crotch with a knee, he tried to think quickly of the boxing lessons he'd taken at the Mission Club House a long time ago.

He hit Roman hard in the belly; he felt his fist sink into the doughlike fat, heard the man's blast of expelled breath. They skidded on the mud, struggling to gain purchase with their feet. Roman was a ruffian, fighting without finesse, depending on brute strength and cowardly traps. Charlie watched the round skull, hard as a bullet, the blunt bevel of his shoulders with the pads of soft fat which lay along the upper arms. He trapped both of Roman's arms under his elbows and jerked his head away in the nick of time as the other's skull jabbed upwards at his chin, while around them the hangers-on yelled and whooped and danced up and down in their excitement.

Charlie moved back and hooked a punch into Roman's kidneys and another into the fat-layered belly, then danced away. The mud sucked and grasped at his boots.

Roman shook his head, his mouth open showing a pink O behind the dark lips, sucking for wind. He cursed and stamped the mud in fury, then shuffled forward across the churned ground, feinted with his body to lure Charlie in. He dropped his arms and rushed forward, his body open, his blunt head down. Charlie tried again for the belly, missed, and then before he could swing clear, was hurled back on his heels by a savage punch he had not seen.

His arms windmilled for balance, but he was going down and thrust out a hand to avoid smacking into the soft mud. He struck the ground on hip and flat of one hand, and lurched clear just as Roman swung at his head with a booted foot. Charlie seized the foot, levering himself up onto his own feet, and brought Roman down. The thick man struck the ground with a liquid thud, and after that he was a cursing, kicking, striking ball of fury.

Charlie plodded away, breathing hard, furious at the slithery ground underfoot, watching Roman rise. They circled each other like terriers. Charlie feinted, and then hit the other, left and right, in the belly, bringing Roman's guard down. He got another hard blow in, before Roman reached and fastened on him. The black, cropped skull jerked at his face, and he twitched his head away, feeling the curved bone, hard as a tyre rim, graze his jawbone, bringing a flash of pain that made his eyes sting. He broke away, blinking against tears.

A spasm of rain came suddenly, splashed the square, hesitated and then passed on. It left little craters in the surface of the mud and filled the puddles into miniature floods. The sky had a flat, battle-grey look.

Roman growled breathlessly: "Hold still and fight right, man." He wheezed for air, like a man trapped in a sealed tomb. Liquor and tobacco had winded him. He came in again, shambling through the brown wetness under his feet. Charlie moved up, his fists working in small, tight, predatory circles. He wanted to get this fight over. He drove at Roman's body and saw the retching look in the stubbled face. Roman reached for him, but Charlie spun aside, saw his chance and struck again. Roman's softness was creeping up, unable to hide behind the wide-sprung mouth and unclear eyes, the greyness under the dark, pouchy skin. He seemed to surrender to helplessness, for he waggled his head and dropped his arms. Charlie started in, then feinted back as Roman, hoping he had fallen into the trap, came to life with an effort and struck out. He missed, and, off balance, stumbled forward, and Charlie, dancing in again, struck with a short, hard, fist-numbing, up-cutting blow, feeling the knuckles collide painfully with the bristly chin. Roman grunted and then made a sighing sound, feeling his head rattle like a stale nut, and hearing somewhere far off the shouting of the on-lookers. Then power snapped out of him like a fused light, and he fell awkwardly to the mud, his cheek smacking the wetness.

The group of disreputable spectators were yelling, prancing in the mud, and Charlie stepped back, breathing hard and shaking his head to clear it. He stood still, gathering his breath, reaching for the slicker, while near him a boy in a torn shirt and three-quarter pants was shadow-boxing in the mud, saying gleefully, "Just like that, *mos*. One, two, one, two. Don't I say? Just like that, oh boy."

Charlie said, wiping mud from the legs of his jeans: "Tell him to leave my little brother alone, understand? What he want to mess with us for?" The others were gathered around the fallen Roman, and did not look at Charlie as he moved off.

Chapter Seven

A small wind blew across the settlement and picked up its smell of mould and the stench of the gaping latrines, the scent of fertile earth and dead leaves, and carried some away with it. Overhead the sky erected its fortresses of granite-grey clouds and brandished its threat of rain.

Down a muddy trail between crooked rows of shacks came a band of children. They scrambled and hopped, spun and cavorted in a sort of dilapidated ballet of wretchedness, shrieking and cheering, laughing with mucous-smeared, goblin faces and the colourless eyes of poverty. Arms like the loosely-joined parts of a construction-set flapped and wobbled as they beat the moisture-laden air, their feet and legs lapping at the black mud as if sucking in some horrid jelly. Around them a troop of curs yelped in a shrill counterpoint.

In the midst of the crowd of children and dogs was a woman, a squalid parody of a female, crowing with drunken laughter, lurching and stumbling along, as if a shopwindow dummy had first been abandoned for years in a sewer, then rescued, crudely stuffed with odds and ends, dressed in a gown of sewn-up dish-rags, and finally, with the use of some faulty clockwork, made to walk.

Around her the children laughed and mocked, pulling at the rag-taggle dress, pelting her with mud, and skipping away with the agility of monkeys whenever she clawed and struck out at them with her drunken hands.

"Drunk 'Ria. Drunk 'Ria," the children sang around her.

"Wah-lah, *ou* drunk 'Ria. Drunk 'Ria."

The woman, hideous as a witch, lurched and stumbled, fell into the mud, picked herself up under the storm of clods, wept, cursed, laughed, shrieked, tottered onward, fell again.

"Drunk 'Ria. Drunk 'Ria."

Along the lane the inhabitants of the tin shanties came to their dooryards and shoo-ed the children, scolding them when ignored, and then joined in the laughter at the woman's inebriated antics.

"Oh, God, 'Ria's at it again."

"Wa-allah, *ou* drunk 'Ria."

"And so, 'Ria? Where are you off to this morning?"

"Stop it, hold your mouths, you rude children. He. He. He."

"*Ou* drunk 'Ria. Drunk 'Ria."

"Isn't it a scandal, hey? Look at her. Ha. Ha. Ha."

"Drunk 'Ria. Drunk 'Ria. Drunk 'Ria."

Laughing and jeering with the viciousness only children know, the crowd made its way down the lane. Now and then they scattered as the drunken woman lashed out at them, cursing horribly, or tripped over their feet. Her hair straggled like wet and dirty straw, her clothes reeking of wine and vomit, and she cursed and wept and laughed about her in a voice as harsh as a death-rattle.

Chapter Eight

Charlie Pauls turned into the track on his way towards the main road, and saw the woman leaning on the gnarled gatepost before the tiny cabin. The gatepost was one end of the haphazard fence constructed out of odd bits of wire joined together and strung along a row of peeled branches stuck into the ground. The wire rested on forks and notches in the poles, and because none of them were level, the wire straggled up and down like crude graphwork. The tiny lot was grown with weeds, dark-green and frightening, and a partly-moulted chicken bobbed and pecked its way through it. The cabin itself was lowroofed, little more than a hut, of the ubiquitous flattened tin-cans and rusty sheet-iron. Charlie saw the woman from the end of the track and made his way towards her.

There was mud on Charlie's trousers and shirt and he slapped at it, picking at congealed patches as he stepped carefully across the ruts that overflowed with dark water. A procession of mongrels of various and nondescript colours circled cautiously around a bitch, growling at each other in their throats. Charlie was thinking, That blerry Ronny, he is going to get into big trouble yet, if he don't hold his head. He carried the yellow slicker over one arm, while he picked at the mud with his free hand. He shivered a little in the cold, and from the delayed shock of the fight. But now, coming up to the woman, he smiled, pleased to see her there.

"Where are you walking around, Charles?" the woman asked, from the gateway. "Look at yourself. There's mud on your clothes. Did you slip?"

"Morning, Freda. How goes it?" Charlie said, still brushing at the mud. "I'm going up to that garage up there. Mostert." Earth fell from his clothes, but dark smears remained. "No, I didn't fall. Is nothing."

Freda said, smiling gently: "You been scarce, hey." And Charlie said with forced casualness, "I been busy. How you been, Freda?"

"Oh, so-so," she told him, and added: "You better come inside and wash that mud off."

Charlie said, "Ah, is nothing, man."

He smiled at her. She was a good-looking woman, he thought. She was thickly built, but soft and big-breasted and big-hipped under the soiled and faded overall she wore. The overall was dark over the heavy breasts. She had thick eyebrows and a broad, kindly, heavy face, the full lips soft, and her coarse black hair was tied back with a scrap of cloth.

Then she saw the swelling graze on the side of his jaw. "Look at your face, man. Look like you been fighting." Her face softened with concern. "Did you fight? Come in, man. I got some salve for that."

"Hell, is nothing," Charlie said, but he went in through the sagging gateway. And seeing again the sturdy legs and the shapes of the strong hips under the overall dress, he thought with a twinge of desire of the times he had slept in the shack. Her own husband had died in a lorry smash two years ago, and Charlie had a suspicion that she now expected him to marry her.

Two children in ragged clothes sat in the doorway, chewing at thick slices of bread, moving aside to let them in. The woman said, "Go play, you children," and

56

they got up and edged into the weeds, chewing silently.

Charlie went inside behind the woman, drawing down his head to clear the low doorway. He asked, "You not working today, Freda?" straightening a little as he crossed the threshold to come into the room.

"You know *mos* I only work three days a week," she said. "I'll get some water. Wait a little. Sit down so long."

Charlie said, "I'll dirty the place if I sit. I'll just stand till we get this mud off."

The room was low-ceilinged, and cramped, like most of the rest of the shacks, the uneven floor of dung and packed earth covered with cheap oilcloth which had worn out long ago, particularly across the bumps between the hollows. A curtain, sagging on a length of string, divided the room in two, and a cheap kitchen dresser was propped against the wall in one corner, and next to it a small table laden with chipped crockery and a primus stove, and a big metal can which held the water that had to be fetched every day from the communal taps.

Between Charlie and the curtain stood an old oval table, one of its legs propped with a block of wood, and on it a hideous plasterware bowl, its paint cracked and chipped, showed its dirty white insides like scabless dead flesh. An old rickety, wooden settee against the wall opposite the dresser made up the rest of the furniture, and above it, hanging from a crooked nail, a dusty frame containing a badly-coloured, double-portrait of a tinted Freda in a wedding veil and a man with a blank, ludicrously yellow face and a moustache like a pinch of pepper, a striped collar, who had been her husband. Stuck in the frame was a sidewalk snapshot of Freda, looking older and smiling, and posing with a shopping-bag. The room smelled warmly of cooking, paper and soap.

Charlie stood by the table and peered past the old-fashioned lamp that hung from the branch pole and cardboard ceiling, and he said: "You mustn't waste the water, girl," while he stood there, holding the yellow slicker, and the sky sagged heavily with rain heads behind him, beyond the doorway.

She came back, carrying a tin bowl she had filled from the container on the table, and he saw again her loose-hipped movement and the quiver of the swollen breasts under the overall, and he smiled at her.

"I really missed you, Freda," he said.

She put the bowl on the table and said, "*Garn.* Is that why you never came around?" She stood near him, one hand holding the shirt stretched, while she dabbed at the mud, and he could smell the warm, sweaty scent of her body and feel her breath hot on his neck. Freda squeezed out the cloth in the dish and said: "Why did you fight? Is not nice to fight in the street, *mos.*"

He looked at her and said, with a little pride: "They was interfering with my brother. A man must *mos* fight for his brother, don't I say?"

She scrubbed away at the muddy shirt and then at the jeans, and looking down he saw the smooth, brown, blue-veined flesh of her breasts. He put an arm around her shoulders and she straightened, moving from him, her eyes bright. But she said, softly: "Hey, don't be so touchy."

He was a man of salacious good humour, and he said, smiling: "Oh, Freda, I touched lots of your places before."

"Shut up," she said, and there was a flush under the brown colour of her face. "You think you can come here anytime you like, then keep yourself funny?" She went away from him to the dresser and he said after her: "You got another friend, Freda?" He sounded a little anxious.

"What you think I am?" she flashed back, annoyed. She found a little jar of petroleum jelly and unscrewed the cap.

Charlie said, gently, "Awright, *bokkie*. Awright, don't get so *dingus*."

Outside, the sky blackened suddenly and the rain came down. They could hear the rain scouring the roof and sputtering in the muddy tracks around the house. The two children scampered in and stood in the doorway, watching the rain and holding their crusts. Freda smiled mischievously at Charlie, knowing that the children's presence frustrated any plans he might have for her.

It was dry and warmer inside the hut. The walls had been lined with sheets of cardboard from grocery cartons and papered with strips from a printer's dump, so that one could read parts of advertisements and coloured labels as one sat there in the primus-warmth.

"Give me that," Charlie said, taking the ointment jar from her. "I can put it on myself. You reckon I'm a baby?" He looked at her, scowling a little, and then out towards the sheeting rain. "I got to get up to the garage. Got to get something to mend the roof." He winced softly as he fingered jelly onto the graze on his face.

Freda said: "I want you to mend the primus. It don't burn properly. Goes on and off likely."

Charlie went over and picked up the stove, shook it, holding it near an ear. One of its legs had broken off and had to be propped up to make it stand. "Maybe blocked," he said. "I'll take a look soon's I come around again." He put it back on the table and it stood lopsided on two legs.

Freda said, "Wait a little till the rain stop. Sit down, all the mud's off."

He grinned. "You really want *ou* Charlie to sit down, hey?"

She folded her thick, smooth arms under her breasts and said with gentle cajolery, avoiding his eyes purposely, "You can do as you please." He grinned again and sat down on the settee, and then she seemed to remember something, and turned back to the dresser, opened its cupboard door and drew out a flat bottle. She held it up to the light and Charlie saw that it was almost half-full of brandy.

Freda said, "There. Look what I even kept for you. I thought you'd come around, and it standing here all the time." She took a thick tumbler from a shelf.

Charlie said, smiling: "*Howkees,* Freda, *bokkie*, little goat. That's real smart of you, *mos*."

"I brought it from the missus weeks ago. Found it on the master's desk. They got lots, they won't miss it." She put the bottle and the glass on the table.

"Sit down here by me, *bokkie*," Charlie said. But she smiled and went to stand by the children at the door, watching the rain.

"Look like eight-day rain," she said.

"Ah, it will stop and then start, on and off," Charlie said with authority, as he unscrewed the cap of the bottle. "Eight-day won't start yet."

She turned and leaned against the doorpost, her arms folded, watching him. "Sometimes it's two weeks of rain."

Charlie poured some of the brandy into the glass. "Nothing like a little *brandewyn* to warm the blood, hey?" And he smiled at her, lasciviously. "You going to have a *doppie,* a drink?"

"You know I don't drink."

"Ah, come on, *bok,* just one. Come on."

"Don't be funny. Have your *dring.*"

He smiled and let his eyes run over her. She tossed her head and looked away, and he laughed while she watched the screen of grey water. He said, "*Gesond-heid,*" and tossed off the brandy. The strong liquor slid down his throat, burning all the way, and spread warmly in his stomach, and then he felt the pleasant sensation creep gently through his body. He drew out his cigarette tin and lighted up. He poured another drink and said, sincerely, "Nice of you to keep a man a *dring,* Freda. That white boss of yours keep real wake-up brandy."

"I thought you'd come round a long time awready."

He said, smiling, "I tell you what, I'll leave a little in the bottle and I'll come and finish it later."

She said scornfully, "Huh."

"You'll see. I'll come and see you more often, Fredie." He picked up the second drink and said, "Luck, Fredie."

Outside the hut, the rain hissed and gurgled, and with the second brandy came desire, and he looked at the woman, smiling happily, and allowing the knot of desire to swell inside him, opening like a blooming flower. He began to think of the nights he'd spent behind the curtain with her. The children crouched at the door and looked out into the rain, and he thought, Oh, dammit, dammit. But there was something more than desire for her inside him, and it worried him a little.

Freda turned away from the door, saying to the

children, "Don't you go into the rain, hear?" and as she moved near, Charlie grabbed recklessly at her, gripping an arm.

"Freda, Freda," he laughed, feeling slightly drunk from two brandies. The other hand reached for a full, rounded buttock, but she twisted out of his grasp.

"Charles, man. You see the children are here." She rubbed the spot on her arm where he had gripped her. "You so rough also."

He was standing up now, with sex curling and uncurling like a worm inside himself. He said, shakily, "Oh, bugger the lighties. Come on. Please."

"What you think I am? One of your bad women?"

"My bad women? What you mean *my* bad women, *bokkie*, little goat?" He laughed at her. The children looked around and giggled, huddling together. He said, "We could send them for water, or to the shop or *dingus*."

"No." Her voice was firm, and he submitted, knowing that she was not a whore, and that it was not because of that she had given herself to him in the past. So he smiled at her, feeling crude lust shrivel and die like a burnt-out match, leaving only the slight, pleasant drunkenness.

She stood with a hip against the oval table and made marks on its dull surface with the tip of one rough finger, while Charlie pulled on his yellow slicker. He gazed at her standing by the ugly, chipped, plaster flower bowl, and said, "You keep me this *dop* of brandy, hey?" He realised suddenly that the rain had stopped again. "Well, I better make quick up to *ou* Mostert."

He reached out and patted a shoulder gently, without lust, and she did not try to avoid him, but said quietly, "You not going to stay away so long again?"

He said, "I'll be back quick-quick. True as God. You'll see."

They went to the door together and he paused before he ducked out, then cried, "So long, Fredie," and then he was leaping the flooded pathway.

The curdled grey sky hung bloated with moisture, and the landscape between the wet cabins shone with archipelagoes of pools. Charlie hurried up the lane, feeling warm under the yellow slicker, and did not mind the water soaking through his boots as he sloshed through the unavoidable mire.

Freda watched him go, until he had disappeared. Then she went back into the room, picked up the brandy bottle that still held two fingers of liquor in it, and put it away in the cupboard. Then she picked up the basin of muddy water and emptied it through the doorway, and took it back with the glass to the table where she put them with the rest of the dishes that had to be washed up.

The children edged towards the door and she said to them, "Don't you children get wet." When they had dashed out again, into the mud, Freda started to wash the dishes, and now found herself wishing that it had not rained while Charles had been there.

Chapter Nine

The highway from the city unreeled like dark, wet adhesive, pasted like a strip across the country, curving in places where it seemed to have come unstuck from the moist surface of the land. The Service Station and Garage stood just off one of these curves in the road where it navigated a bulge of gum, green portjackson wood and wattle, as it by-passed a string of suburbs.

Like a lone blockhouse on a frontier, it stood against the dark-green background of trees, with an air of neglect surrounding it, as if deserted by its garrison and left to crumble on the edge of hostile territory. Of course, George Mostert, the owner of the Service Station and Garage was always there, but one could hardly consider him part of an occupation; he was more like a volunteer who had agreed to, or had been ordered into standing a lone rearguard action. The rash of new, modern service stations which had sprung up in and nearer the city over the years had blighted his trade, and the traffic going north flashed past him, their tanks already filled and their tyres inflated, while the drivers heading towards the city could afford to ignore him, knowing that they did not have to give him their custom because they could usually make it to the end of the journey.

So the place just hung on, its dirty white exterior like an ignored flag of surrender on the road. There was a grease-blackened apron out front, outside the service area, and a row of advertising stands displaying a selection of dusty bottles of lubrication oil. The well of the hoist was full of jet black water, and the hoist itself covered with a thick coat of ancient grease; and the walls of the building looked as if a giant had clutched it with greasy fingers.

It was not a big place, so a stack of worn-out tyres in a corner by the tiny glass office seemed to take up most of the space leading into the small, dim garage. The windows of the office were smudged to such an extent that they looked like frosted glass: a gallery of assorted fingerprints which would have driven a detective insane. And here and there a selection of old coloured stickers and pennants and labels advertising various brands of oils, lubricants, petrol, and long-abandoned novelties for the children of potential customers.

The white paint on the outside of the building had long been violated by the elements and careless drivers. There was history written in the fender-scars and the hub cap marks, the dried-up pools of grease like the congealed blood of dead business, in the chipped and battered enamel signs, and the torn and faded bunting like the shields and pennons of slain enterprise hung up for the last time in forlorn defiance.

For George Mostert stayed on amid the tawdry leftovers of his garage; nobody could explain why. Now and then a spasm of work came, like the last twitches of a dying carcass: flat tyres to be fixed or air-locks in a gas line. Somebody needed a choked carburettor cleaned out or points ground; sometimes one of the old wrecks from among the shanty dwellers was driven up to be hammered and patched and riveted into a precarious roadworthiness, or somebody would even buy a gallon or two of petrol.

George Mostert was somewhere over forty years old. He had been married once, and it was rumoured that his wife, tired of his lack of ambition or his premature surrender to encroaching competition, had run off with a used-car salesman. But George had never spoken to anybody about it, so the rumour had never been verified. Nevertheless, his loneliness hung about him in the form of a spirit of enforced friendliness, a desire for conversation, a willingness to do a small favour. It was in the lines around his insignificant mouth under the bedraggled ginger moustache like a cheap cigar coming apart, and in the puddles of his eyes on each side of his nondescript nose. Solitude clung in the half moons of black grease under his uncut fingernails, and in the wrinkles of his rugose neck, in the dirty overalls and the lank, uncombed, brittle, greying hair the colour of dusty floor-polish. It weighed his shoulders into a limp stoop, and dragged at his feet like shackles. So he pottered around the service station like a stray dog sniffing at a familiar scent, or peered out through the blurred glass of his office, hoping that a car would pull up on the cracked apron treacherous with dirty oil, so that he could go out and talk to its driver.

At night George Mostert locked up the place and went upstairs to the room over the garage. He did his own cooking – he ordered the groceries over the telephone – and then he would read a battered murder novel or sit at the window and watch the great twelve-wheelers rumble past in the dark, their rows of lights winking like ruby-red eyes as they rushed from him.

From the garage he could also look across the road and see the jumbled pattern of shacks and shanties sprawled like an unplanned design worked with dull rags on a dirty piece of crumbled sack-cloth: a strange country, a foreign people met only through ragged brown ambassadors who stopped by sometimes to beg for some useful rubbish, or called a greeting on their way on some obscure mission.

Beyond the settlement was the rubbish dump with its patrols of flies and its gas defence of stinking decay, and then the first, ruined, rambling plaster houses of the suburb proper: a line of single rooms like adobe huts in a Western film, a huddle of broken cement stoops and sagging verandahs, gradually changing into red-painted roofs and chimneypots, the bulk of a cinema with a broken neon sign, a church tower, a high wall that formed one side of a boot factory.

Life was there, no matter how shabby, a few yards from George Mostert's Service Station and Garage, but he was trapped in his glass office by his own loneliness and a wretched pride in a false racial superiority, the cracked embattlements of his world, and he peered out sadly past the petrol pumps which gazed like petrified sentries across the concrete no-man's-land of the road.

But when he saw Charlie Pauls come up from behind the embankment, his head and shoulders rising above the concrete horizon, George Mostert felt a little stir of pleasure. It was somebody to pass a word to again, although, he thought dismally, the fellow wasn't *his* kind, really. He went out of the dusty glass office onto the greasy apron of the service station.

Charlie Pauls crossed the road, leaving a faint trail of muddy prints behind him. He was still feeling warm inside, and a little happy from the two tots of brandy he had drunk, and he was thinking, Well, she's not a bad piece. He came onto the space behind the petrol pumps and smiled at the garage owner.

He said, "Morning, Mister George."

"Morning," George Mostert returned. He had seen Charlie around before, and had passed the time of day with him, and once he had allowed him to carry away some scrap metal. He added, cautiously, "How's things?"

Charlie gazed around the place. He said, "So-so, Mister George." Then he looked directly at George Mostert and went on: "I say, Mister George, I must ask you another pleasure. Other time you give me some scrap to fix up the house. Now the blerry roof is leaking. Rain coming into the blerry house. Well, I reckon, you *mos* give me that stuff last time –"

George Mostert sensed the praise and he cut in, "You want some more scrap?"

"If you can spare it, Mister George." Charlie knew that there was a whole yard full of junk behind the building, but he talked as if he was asking a great favour of George Mostert, so that the man was trapped by a feeling of magnanimity.

George Mostert drew a soiled handkerchief from his overall pocket and blew his nose. He said, dabbing: "Well, I reckon there might be some. But you people took most of the good stuff away. Now there's just motor-car parts and things lying around." He added, "Jesus, it's like your whole bloody – ah – village is built from the stuff you get here."

Charlie grinned and gestured with his large hands. "Hell," he said. "They ought to make you the may-or, Mister George."

Mostert glanced at him and could not resist the faint glow-worm flicker of pride that fluttered in his breast. He smiled and wiped his nose again and led the way around the building towards the back area, Charlie trailing behind him.

Charlie said, boldly, "I say, Mister George, you *mos* all alone up here. Don't I say? You must come over one day and we can fix up something, *mos*."

"Something?"

"A kin' of a party, *mos,* Mister George," Charlie told him, walking across the atolls of grease with the faded man. "We can quickly fix up a few cans. Have a nice drink, *mos*."

George Mostert said, quickly: "I don't want any trouble."

"Ahhh," Charlie said. "Trouble. You scared of trouble? But I don't reckon there going to be trouble. You haven't got a wife, hey, Mister George?"

"No."

A drop of moisture fell from the sky and hit Charlie's neck. He wiped it away and peered up at the sky. "Going to rain. Must fix the roof before she come down." Then he reverted back to the previous discussion. "Right. A couple of cans and some talking and singing. People got a right to have some pleasure, don't I say?" He laughed and shook his head.

They came around the back of the service station. "Listen, Mister George, and excuse me for saying so. I know what's worrying you. But we *mos* men of the world." He grinned and winked. "I tell you, I was in Egypt with the war. Had me a French goose in Alexandria. *She* didn't min' what colour men she took in. All the blerry same to *her*."

George Mostert looked a little shocked and ashamed at hearing a white woman talked about in this way. He said, hurriedly: "Well, you better pick out what you want."

"Thanks, Mister George."

They were facing an area of piled and scattered metal

debris. It was as if all the leaving of a modern battle-field had been collected and dumped there: heaped and entangled rusty and broken automobile engines, chassis, fenders, struts, mudguards, radiators, spring-leaves, axles, wheels, coach-work, detached doors, bolts and seat-springs, all the abandoned offal from butchered traffic lay in the yard, flaking with brown rust, clogged with a paste of sand and oil and grease.

Charlie stalked among the dead husks of one-time transport, and George Mostert thought, tentatively, It doesn't sound like a bad idea having a good time with them. Nobody would see. Only, well only, it looked so bloody dirty and mucky. Christ, having a good time in the middle of all that muck. Loneliness speared him, and he winced inwardly at the bitter wounding. He shambled after Charlie, as if the coloured man's proximity would compensate for what he might have to forgo.

"Man, Mister George," Charlie said, wandering through the terrain of rusting metal. "Man, you could put some of these parts together and fix up a blerry car for yourself."

"I've got a car," George Mostert said. "Chev. You know about cars?"

Charlie squatted on his heels and looked under the bodyless wreck of a coupe. "Learned about motors in the army. I was a transport driver." He peered into the bottom of the engine. "Some good parts left here, I reckon." He rose and slapped the rusted metal affectionately. Then he remembered what he had come for and started to walk around with intent, moving chipped canopies and engine bonnets. George Mostert shuffled after him.

George Mostert said, cautiously, "Say, you think it would be awright if I slipped down there one evening?"

"Where?" Charlie asked, not looking at him, but examining old scraps of fenders and lengths of metal, measuring them for size with his eyes. "You mean down there by us? Any time, Mister Mostert, any time."

"Help yourself," George Mostert said. "Maybe I'll come along, hey?" And he went on with a twinge of desperation: "I could buy a couple of cans myself and bring them with me."

Charlie moved a sheet of iron with a booted foot and grinned at him: "Okay, Mister George. That will be fix-up, *mos*. When you coming, hey?"

George Mostert plunged recklessly on. "Saturday night," he said. He wiped his nose on his soiled handkerchief. He thought he had a cold coming on. "I'll be down Saturday night. Okay?"

"I reckon that will be class, Mister George," Charlie said. "Saturday nights is when things are wake-up down there."

Now he had found a section of sheet-metal he thought would do for the damaged roof, partly bent and just a little rusted, but still in condition to last a long time. He started to drag it through the maze of wreckage towards the end of the yard, with George Mostert shambling behind him, sniffing.

"You can have that," George Mostert said with a wet smile. "You got to let me know where to come."

Charlie dropped the end of the tin-plate in the wet soil and pointed across the road towards where he had emerged when he had come up to the service station. He said, "Right over there is a kind of path down through the houses. You go straight, you see, Mister George." He gave directions and the other man listened, watching the indicating hand with his red-rimmed, washed-out eyes. He felt like a man who had decided to undertake some desperate adventure: an explorer who had summoned up courage to enter a territory never yet trodden by man. His heart beat hollowly under his grease-stained overalls and he hoped he would not develop a cold. He would take a stiff shot of brandy as soon as he got inside. It did not occur to him to offer Charlie a shot, too.

George Mostert watched the yellow-slickered figure cross the road and disappear down the embankment, leaving only his muddy footprints on the concrete to mark his going. Then he started back towards the windowed office under the canopy of the service station.

He sat down at the little desk piled with dusty papers, dog-eared accounts, towers of receipts stuck on wire spikes, pamphlets showing engine parts. A half-eaten sandwich – what was left of his breakfast – lay in a saucer, sponging up a dusty puddle of tea. He rummaged in a drawer and found a bottle half-full of brandy and poured a stiff drink into the teacup without bothering to empty out the dregs. He drank down the liquor quickly, gagged and swallowed, feeling his eyes smart.

A car went by with a roar of tyres on concrete, a big blue sedan with stainless-steel fittings half-bright under the wet sky. George Mostert watched its swift passing and sneered faintly, with a new-found bravado. He pulled his handkerchief from his pocket, found a dry spot on it, and blew his nose vigorously.

Chapter Ten

When Charlie Pauls reached home he put the sheet of metal he had brought from Mostert's against the side of the house and walked around into the yard. Overhead the heavy sky strained under its incalculable weight of rain. In the door of the packing-case shack in the yard stood Caroline, Charlie's sister. She smiled at him shyly as he appeared, and moved gently, shifting from one foot to the other.

She said, "Morning, Charlie."

He smiled at her. Caroline was seventeen, married and great with pregnancy. Her hair was awry, un-combed, a tangled bundle around her head and brown-blotched, woman-child face with its dumb, calf-like eyes. She had a well-developed body, and with her pregnancy she looked older than she was. Caroline was shy and withdrawn, and Charlie even thought she was a little simple-minded. She smiled readily, but vacantly, spoke in a quiet voice, and then usually when she was addressed first. When she was required to do anything, she had to be given explicit instructions and went about the task dully and without emotion, as if a machine had been wound up and set to perform an automatic function.

Charlie liked her, but he always felt a certain embar-rassment, and often had a feeling that she contained some sort of insoluble mystery.

Alfred, her eighteen-year-old husband saw nothing

peculiar about Caroline, and when he was not fawning over her or slyly showing off his mature-bodied wife to other men, he regarded her with a mixture of awe and passion.

Now Charlie said, smiling at her: "Hell, Ca'line, you getting bigger and bigger every day. Bet you'll bust, too."

And Caroline giggled foolishly, and lowered her eyes, shifting again on her feet.

"Your roof okay? Not leaking?" Charlie asked.

"Is awright," the girl answered, in her quiet tone. "Alfy say is okay."

"Alfy," Charlie grunted. "There's only one thing awright, as far as that bugger's concerned." And he grinned again, lasciviously, then asked: "You people heard from the Council yet about a house?"

"Alfy said they said he don't get enough money," the girl burst out. "They reckon we can only get a house when he get more money." She shut her lips as soon as the words were out, as if disconcerted by the speech she had made.

". . ." Charlie said, and smiled at her again. "Never min', *ou* girl. You's *mos* here with us, hey?" He took out his tin and lighted a cigarette. "Well, I got to try and fix up our roof." He asked, "How's the *ou kerel*, old man, been while I was gone?"

"He's still sick," Caroline answered. She folded her hands protectively over her great abdomen, leaning against the side of the opening in the shack, and watched him stroll over to the Pauls house.

From behind the curtained doorway came the moaning of the sick old man, like the far-away lowing of a fog-horn. Ma Pauls came out of the room into the kitchen. She was wearing a shabby coat over her dress, and her eyes were weary under the black head-cloth.

Charlie asked, "How's Dad, Ma?"

"He's getting weaker, Charles. He must have a doctor, really."

"You going for the doctor? I could have gone."

"No," Ma said. "Not the doctor. We owe the doctor, and he said last time he won't come till we pay cash. And there's no money till Ronny get pay Friday." She buttoned her coat. "I'm going up to Mulela for some herbs. Maybe the herbs will help." She walked to the door. "You stay around and look after the *ou kerel*."

Charlie said, "Okay, Ma. But you got to make quick, it might rain again."

"I will hurry."

"I got to go on the roof again. Got a piece of iron from Mostert's."

"Awright. But you mustn't make a noise, hear?"

"Ca'line can sit by Dad so long."

"She can. But she wouldn't know what to do. You wouldn't neither, I reckon. But I'll make haste. You just watch him."

In the bedroom Dad Pauls wheezed and muttered, like a motor running down. Overhead the dish-rag-coloured sky swelled with rain. But on the shuddering roof of the shanty Charlie carefully ripped away rotten tin. The shanty creaked and sagged dangerously, and Charlie worked with anxiety, afraid that the whole roof might collapse under him. A few big drops of moisture fell, tapping on the hard oilskin of his slicker, and he looked quickly up at the drab threat of the sky. He manhandled the sheet of metal he had brought from Mostert's service station, working it under the edges of the hole he had made in the roof, cursing under his breath as jagged shark's teeth scraped his knuckles.

He was still busy jamming the sheet into position when his Uncle Ben came around the leaning side of the house and saw him.

"Hullo, Charlie-boy. Roof got holes?"

Charlie looked over the edge of the roof, sucking his torn knuckles. He said, "*Hoit,* Uncle Ben. Leaking. How goes it?" He frowned at the raw gash. "Don't you work today?"

"Weather," Uncle Ben said upward. "Painters can't work in the rain, so we laid off. Another day lost, I reckon."

Uncle Ben was a short, tubby man; a dark, half-burnt dumpling dressed in a holed jersey and shiny, worn and patched trousers. His shoes were cracked and muddy, and had been slit over his bunions, and in spite of the cheerful rotundity of his body, the dark eyes in their puffy sockets had an expression of resignation to some inexplicable woe. His face was shiny and loosefleshed from too much drinking, and his mouth had a moist redness of lip, like the trace of a clumsy kiss. He carried paint-stained overalls, tattered, bundled into a parcel under one arm, and wore an old, paint-hardened felt hat on his greying, steel-wool head.

Charlie said to him: "There's some rocks there next to the fence. You reckon you can give me up one at a time, Uncle Ben? Can't hit no nails into the roof, now. Old Dad's very sick inside."

"Sure, Charlie-boy," Uncle Ben said. He put his bundle down carefully on a mound of earth, and bent, grunting and straining against his intervening paunch. "How *is* your pa, Charlie?" He heaved a rock upwards and Charlie reached it onto the roof.

"Bad, Uncle Ben, bad," Charlie told him. "But bad."

"I thought I'd come around and see the old boy, *mos.*

I reckoned he'd be bad in this weather." Another rock was raised. They talked while Uncle Ben handed up the rocks.

"Your Ma must have her hands full, poor old lady."

"*Ja*, I reckon so. Don't let it fall, *oomie*. If I could find a job, it wouldn't be so bad, *mos*."

"Hold on, boy. Dammit, almost dropped this one. I thought you was working on the road up by whatchacallit – Calvinia."

"It was just a contrack job," Charlie said. "A month for one-pound-twelve-and-six a week. We came home when it was finish."

"*Ja*," Uncle Ben sighed. "It goes like that, *mos*. I just been doing odd jobs. Few bob here, few bob there."

Charlie was moving the heavy stones about the roof, weighing down the tin where gaps showed. He said down to his uncle: "You *can mos* go inside and see the old man so long. I'm almost finish here."

Uncle Ben asked with some anxiety: "Your Ma by the house?"

Charlie grinned. He said, "No. She's gone out for herbs for Dad."

"Well, I'll go inside, then."

Charlie chuckled to himself and watched Uncle Ben pick up his bundle, and holding it with care, go around the house. Uncle Ben kept out of Ma Paul's way as much as possible, because she was against his excessive drinking and was always lecturing about it. Uncle Ben was Ma's brother, and he lived in a little shack somewhere in the settlement. He hadn't married, and lived alone, drinking away most of the little money he earned doing odd house-painting jobs. Charlie had an idea what Uncle Ben had wrapped up in his overall.

While he was moving the last rock into position, the

sky flapped open and the rain began. It whisked on the roof and drove into Charlie with ferocity. It splashed high in the yard, sheeting down and obscuring the landscape so that the stunted gum and portjackson trees and sprawling shanties merged into one blurred shadow. Charlie clambered from the roof, and stepping from the rickety trestle against the wall, ripped the yellow oilskin on an edge of tin, cursing as he tore himself hurriedly loose. He darted around a corner of the shack and made for the kitchen door.

Chapter Eleven

Jesus," Charlie gasped when he was in the kitchen. I hope the old lady don't get caught in this rain." He pulled off the oilskin slicker. Around the house the rain roared and drummed and the sky was harsh with iron greyness. In the yard the water filled the hollows and washed around the bole of the old mulberry and swirled around the fence-poles and the corner-stones of the shack, sucking at the sand on which they rested, so that the concrete lumps subsided and the whole construction creaked soggily, its weight searching for support.

Charlie shook out the slicker and it flop-flopped water onto the kitchen floor. The dog, Watchman, scrambled through the doorway out of the rain and added to the gathering mud on the worn floorboards. The dog shook itself and crawled into a gap beside the stove. Outside, the weather continued to growl like a hungry monster.

Uncle Ben came from behind the curtain of Dad Pauls' room into the kitchen. "Poor *ou* man," he said. "Blerry sick, *ou* Charlie, blerry sick."

Charlie said, examining the warped cardboard ceiling: "You telling me. I hope the old girl isn't walking in this rain. You better stay here till it hold up, Uncle Ben." He seemed satisfied with the ceiling. "She'll keep, I reckon. Better look in the other room. You see any leaking in Dad's room? I don't like to walk in and out there."

"It look awright," Uncle Ben said. His bundled overall was on the little kitchen table, and now he placed his hands upon it, as if in benediction. "I say, Charlie-boy," he said, softly. "I brought a little something with me. Two of the sweet white. You reckon we could just have a quick one here?"

"Why not?" Charlie said. "We better sit in our room." He grinned at Uncle Ben and winked. Then he led the way. He had hung the slicker on a nail near, but away from, the still warm fire. Uncle Ben followed him, carrying his bundle and disreputable hat.

In the small, cold room the leak in the ceiling had stopped and there was only a wet, spreading stain across the sagging cardboard. Charlie was scared the leak would move to another part of the house, or emerge in several parts. He stood there for a moment with the old smell of food and bedding and damp mould, with the wind whistling through the nail-holes in the walls, and the rain drumming against the house outside.

"You sit on Ronny's bed," he told Uncle Ben. He had brought two pickle jars from the kitchen with him and set them on the box between the beds. Uncle Ben unwrapped his overall reverently, revealing the bottles of wine, and said: "Nothing like a drink on a day like this, hey?" He unscrewed the cap off one of the bottles and poured the yellow liquor into the jars. A thought struck him, and he looked up anxiously at Charlie: "I say, Charles, you reckon your Ma is going to *skel* us out for drink?"

Charlie took one of the jars and looked at the wine in it. He said, seriously: "Ma don't objeck much to drinking, man. Is just you always getting fall-fall drunk. Always falling around, man."

Uncle Ben regarded his own drink, broodingly. He said: "I don't know what it is, Charlie, man. A man got to have his *dring,* don't I say? But with me is like as if something force me to drink, drink, drink. Is like an evil, Charlie, forcing a man to go on swallowing till he's fall-fall with liquor. An evil, man."

A rush of rain scoured the roof and passed on, leaving a gap of silence through the steadier downpour, and then another burst took its place. In the sick-room Dad Pauls moaned tortuously.

"I heard temperance people say drinking is evil," Charlie said.

"I don't mean like that," Uncle Ben said, as they drank the wine. "Is an evil, Charlie, what make a man drink himself to death with wine, an evil what make a poor old man shiver and shake himself to death in a leaking *pondok* without no warm soup and no medicine."

"You think Dad will die?" Charlie asked, in alarm.

"I don't say so," Uncle Ben said, morosely. His drinking bouts were always accompanied by an infinite sadness. "I don't say so. But what make a man got to suffer things? The poor shivering and shaking themselves to death."

Charlie said, drinking some wine, "Well, you *mos* belonged to that Lodge. Man learn things there, I reckon."

"Gave up the Lodge long ago, man," Uncle Ben said. He felt the sadness creep up on him. He smoked one of Charlie's cigarettes between sips from his pickle jar, his drink-swollen face shone through the smoke like an insipid sun in a winter sky. "Lodge don't teach a man nothing, that's all I learned. I read the Bible now and then."

Charlie said, "Ma read the Bible every night. It don't make the poor old toppy any better."

"We got to trust in the Lord, Charlie," Uncle Ben said. "Your Ma read the Bible because she got troubles. She got family troubles. You, and your pa sick, and young Ronny going wild, and Ca'line with her body going to have a baby, and everybody poor."

"And you," Charlie laughed, drinking again. "You in the family, too."

The rain had settled down again to a soft puttering against the house. A fly, trapped by winter, crawled along a length of splintery planking and hesitated at the dusty edge of the sheer cliff to the floor far below. Its myriad eyes searched the room and its wings were dully iridescent in the gloom. After its initial hesitation, it launched itself into space, buzzing softly and banking in mid air, it landed on the box between the beds. The fly wiped its wings and its legs, then hopped forward a little, past a cylinder of flicked ash, and then stopped to rub its face with its forelegs. It seemed to tremble with a chill. Then it took off again, skimmed the bed where Uncle Ben sat and looped, heading towards the dim light beyond the tiny window. But it crashed into the pane and dropped away, recovering in mid air, then buzzed ahead to settle on the sleeve of Charlie's shirt. A hand brushed it away and it sailed across the box again, and settled there. It edged cautiously forward under the sound of voices and reached a drop of spilt wine, then it regurgitated into the drop and drank.

Uncle Ben was saying, ". . . is it. I don't know what is it, Charlie." He was lugubrious now, and the wine had sunk in the first bottle and there was about two inches left.

Charlie said, picking up the bottle and emptying it

into a pickle jar, while Uncle Ben uncapped the other: "There was a burg working with us on the pipe. When we was laying pipe up by Calvinia. Know what he say? Always reading newspapers and things. He said to us, the poor don't have to be poor." He took the second bottle and equalised the drinks in the two pickle jars. "This burg say, if the poor people all got together and took everything in the whole blerry world, there wouldn't be poor no more. Funny kind of talk, but it sounded awright," Charlie said.

He continued, warming up: "Further, this rooker say if all the stuff in the world was shared out among everybody, all would have enough to live nice. He reckoned people got to stick together to get this stuff."

Uncle Ben said, frowning: "Sound almost like a sin, that. Bible say you mustn't covet other people's things."

". . ." Charlie said. "This rooker did know what he was talking, I reckon."

"I heard people talking like that," Uncle Ben said. "That's communis' things. Talking against the govverment."

"Listen," Charlie said, as they had another drink. He was feeling voluble. "Listen, Uncle Ben, one time I went up to see Freda up by that people she work for, cleaning and washing. Hell, that people got a house *mos*, big as the effing city hall, almost, and there's an old bitch with purple hair and fat backsides and her husband eating off a table a mile long, with fancy candles and *dingus* on it. And a *juba* like me can't even touch the handle of the front door. You got to go round the back. Eating off nice shiny tables, plenty of roast meat and stuff." Charlie scowled and swallowed some wine. "Bible say love your neighbour, too. Heard that when I was a lighty in Sunday-school."

The fly had overturned and was now drowning in the puddle of wine, its angled legs beating the air frantically, its wings trapped. Outside, the rain had reduced itself to a thin hiss, like escaping gas. Charlie reached out and wiped the fly off the box with the side of a hand. The fly fell onto the floor and lay in the darkness, struggling. In the sick-room Dad Pauls cough-cough-coughed and then wheezed like a broken bellows.

Uncle Ben said, softly: "I just don't know, Charlie-boy. Maybe you young people know better, *mos*." His voice was sad as tears, and he shook his threadbare mind like an old blanket in order to find a lost idea. Beyond them the anaemic day was starting to fade above the drizzle. Charlie poured two more drinks into the jars and they heard the kitchen door scraping and bumping. "There's Ma," Charlie said.

It was Ma, and she looked in around the door, saying: "Was Darra okay?" Then she saw Uncle Ben and her face straightened. "Oh, is you, hey?"

Uncle Ben grinned sheepishly, and then glanced at Charlie, then said, "I came just to see how Frederick was getting on, Rachel."

"Hmmm." Ma's brown eyes, sharp, rusty nails, jabbed the bottles on the box. "I don't want no drunkenness here, hey."

Charlie said, "Ah, we just taking a small *doppie*, Ma. Did you get wet, Ma?"

There was a film of moisture over the old coat. "Just a little. I waited till it went down. Now I must see to your pa." She withdrew her head and they heard her moving about.

Uncle Ben said, "I better be walking, I reckon."

"Man, sit down, sit," Charlie told him, laughing. "Ma not going to eat you up. There's still some left in this barrel." From the kitchen came the clang of the stove. "There he is. Just enough for two more."

Uncle Ben took his pickle jar and raised it. He was feeling sadly drunk, hesitating on the frontier of intoxication and not having more means of crossing it. He said, "*Gesondheit*," and drank, holding the jar with care, one grubby finger poised delicately.

"*Gesondheid*," Charlie replied, and swallowed his own drink.

Now the wine brought an urge of lechery and he lay back on his bed and thought of Freda, trying to conjure up the shape of her body, breasts, hips, pelvis, but it would not appear and he dozed off, still trying.

Uncle Ben got to his feet and rolled up his overall, picked up his ruin of a hat, and went out to the kitchen, lurching just a little, holding his whole body carefully, as if it was an expensive piece of furniture that he dared not scratch.

In the kitchen there was a sharp smell of herbs, and Ma was mixing a brew with hot water. She said, without looking up, "Got some herbs for Fred. It might help."

Uncle Ben sniffed the air and said: "*Ja,* herbs is good. I remember when I had the colic one time. . . ."

Ma said: "You never *did* have colic, man. Don't talk rorbish."

"It felt like the colic that time," Uncle Ben said, frowning and swaying like a tree in the wind. He was nervous in Ma's presence, and he said, "I got to go now." He belched and covered his soft, spongy lips with a spatulate hand.

"Oh, mustn't go," Ma told him. "Have something to eat." She speared him with her terrible eyes, causing him to shrivel inwardly. "I reckon you don't make yourself much to eat by your house."

"Is awright, Rachel," Uncle Ben said, clutching his hat and overalls. "I don't want to be in the way."

"I always said *mos* you had to get married, take a wife."

"I don't want to take no food out of your mouth, woman," Uncle Ben said.

"Is awright," Ma said to him, stirring the brew of herbs. "We got only a little anyway, so one extra won't make a difference. You go and sit in Charlie's room. I'll call you."

She took no further notice of him, and poured the brew over into a scarred enamel jug. Before she carried it in to Dad Pauls, she laid more wood on the fire in the stove. The flames licked around the wood and she moved a pot over the fire, and the fire broke into a little rumble.

Chapter Twelve

In the winter there is no evening, for the night comes quickly, smothering the unresisting daylight under its chill, dark blanket. There was an iciness in the air which drove the poor into their hovels, where they crouched over puttering oil stoves, wood braziers or old iron stoves. They huddled under blankets after the brown bread and coffee had been consumed, and heard the sounds of encroaching night: the rustle of chickens in a broken-down run, the creek-creek-creek of infinite cricket wings being rubbed together, the far-away wuff-wuff of a hound.

On the concrete road, night-traffic swept by, rubber skimming over stippled surface, sounding like sprayed water; headlamps cut cones of yellow light out of the blackness and did not touch the smell of fermenting rubbish that mingled with the live smell of boiled six-penny meat bones, or the dead smell of rusty metal and rotten wood. The lights of high-powered headlamps, surging away in the darkness, did not touch the lights in the shanties, the glow of paraffin lamps or coals embering in a pierced drum. The rich automobile beams swept above the tiny chinks of malnourished light that tried to escape from the sagging shanties, like restless hope scratching at a door. Along the highway the night-traffic spun past and did not notice the tumbledown latrines that circled the listing shacks and shipwrecked people like sharks in a muddy sea. The roadway flickered with intermittent lights, and the night crept close to embrace the cold earth in its dispassionate arms.

Charlie Pauls squatted against the wall by the stove, sitting on his heels, elbows on knees, and one hand holding the enamel plate near his chin, while he scooped turnip stew into his mouth with the spoon held in the other. The small black mole on his right cheekbone moved with the rhythm of his chewing.

It was warmer now, in the kitchen, with the old iron stove murmuring as the wood burned in it, and the kitchen door shut against the drizzle. The air was a little smoky, too, because the wood had been damp. The dog, Watchman, was curled against Charlie's feet, rumbling in his throat as he waited for the scraps that would come after supper.

The drizzle sounded like escaping steam against the side of the house.

Ma said, "I made a little soup from the turnips for the old man. I think he sleeping now."

She stood near Charlie, by the stove, waiting for the men to finish their meal. Ronald; the little boy, Jorny; Uncle Ben, and Caroline's husband, young Alfy, crowded around the table, cramped into the space. Caroline, heavy and awkward with her pregnancy, leaned against the dresser, watching silently, her dull, blotched face contented and immobile with the fixed expression of a doll. She was secretly proud of her husband, and watched him eat, her eyes following every movement he made.

He was a thin and nondescript young man, with a face that was marked with a blurred anonymity, like a rubber stamp which had moved on a paper, leaving an illegible smudge: an indescribable face in the grey mass of a crowd picture. But he was a hard worker, and a

88

good husband, and at that time overawed by the result of his recently discovered prowess in the marriage bed. He seldom spoke in the company of others, and only Caroline knew what topics of conversation were raised between them in the packing-crate shack in the yard.

Now Charlie said to him, chewing while he spoke: "Your roof must *mos* be holding okay with that tar-paper on it, *ou* Alfy."

"Is awright," Alfy muttered, without looking up from his plate.

"Ca'line reckons youse not going to get one of that houses."

Alfy did not reply, and Ma said, sternly: "I wish you won't talk with your mouth full, Charles."

Charlie swallowed and said, "Sorry, Ma." Then he went on: "Is funny there got to be a lot of people like us, worrying about the blerry roof everytime it rain, and there's other people don't have to worry a damn. Living in wake-up houses like that house Freda work by, like I was telling Uncle Ben, or even just up the road here." He scooped the last spoonful of stew into his mouth, then broke off a piece of bread and began to mop up the bottom of the plate with it. "Some people got no money, some people got a little money, some people got little more money, and other people got a helluva lot. Rooker I was working with laying that pipe, he reckon poor people ought to form a union, likely." He popped the bread into his mouth and chewed.

Ma said, "We all got our burden to bear."

"That's what I say, *mos*," Uncle Ben said.

"*Ja*," Charlie said. "I reckon so. Only, a man *mos* get to reckon and think, who works out how much weight each person got to carry?"

Ma said, "Talking about Freda. How is she?"

"She was awright last time I saw her," Charlie said. "Can I have my cawffee now, Ma?"

While Ma poured black coffee into a cup, Ronald struggled to his feet and clambered away from the table. His mouth was sullen and he had not spoken at all since they had sat down to eat. He glowered at Charlie, who grinned back at him as he made his way towards their room.

Ma asked, frowning at Ronald, "How come you looking so *shel*? What for you looking so sulky?"

But Ronald said nothing, and they heard him banging around in the room.

"I don't know about that boy," Ma said. "Is that girl he going after. She's a bad girl."

Charlie knew the reason for Ronald's surliness. He had taken Ronald aside when he had arrived home from work, and had told him about the man, Roman.

"Listen," Charlie had said. "I don't want to say nothing in front of the old lady, because-why Darra is sick and all that. But that burg, Roman, is laying in your tracks because he reckon you *rommel* with his goose, that Susie Meyer, *mos* . . . ."

And Ronald had flared in his usual way: *"His* goose? Like hell, his goose."

"Listen, man," Charlie had told him. "I reckon he got no real right, he's *mos* married and that, but I had to pull him up myself today, because-why he tried to take it out on me. Well, I can floor him anytime, see? Anytime, so long as he want to move on this family. But he's a hardcase *juba* and I reckon you's a little too light for him. And further, I don't reckon that girl Susie is worth the trouble. Why don't you get some other goose?"

". . ." Ronald had said. "I'm not asking *you* to fight

my battles, understand? You stay out of my business, hey?"

"Okay. But I'm not standing by and see Roman pull up a young brother of mine, don't I say?"

"*Jong*," Ronald had said bitterly. "I can fix Roman myself if I got to, you hear? *Leave* my business alone, man."

"Well, I told him to stop laying on with you. I hope he take that warning."

"Man, I can handle him by myself," Ronald had said and left Charlie.

Now Ma said, wearily: "We tried hard to look after this family, your Dad and me. Now he's sick, bad, and we don't want no more trouble."

Charlie said, "Ah, never min', Ma."

Uncle Ben said, pushing his bench back and rising from the table, "A family always give trouble. People with families have always got troubles, I reckon."

Ma said, "Yes. But I reckon is better to have some troubles than nothing at all." She looked at Uncle Ben.

Charlie swallowed his coffee and got up, too, stretching his legs. The dog, Watchman, slid away among the feet around the table. Charlie said: "You going, Uncle Ben? I'll walk a little way with you."

Ma said, "You going out in this rain, Charles?"

"Is not so bad yet," Charlie told her. He pulled his yellow slicker from the nail and jerked into it. "You haven't got a coat, Uncle," he added.

"Is not far," Uncle Ben said.

Ma said to Charlie: "You take care. There's rough boys what walks around here in the night."

"Hell, I can look after myself."

Uncle Ben said, "Leave him, Rachel. He's *mos* a man, now. Hell, he was seventeen when he join up with the army. Hell of a long time ago, that was, too. Now he's a man."

Charlie grinned at him and winked. Ma said to Uncle Ben, "*Ja*, he's a big man. And I hope he don't turn out like *you*."

Uncle Ben looked sheepish, and Charlie laughed. He said, "Ma, I reckon you just don't know Uncle Ben. What do I say, *oomie*?"

He winked, but Uncle Ben just looked sad, standing there in the smoky light in the kitchen.

Chapter Thirteen

After he had been knocking for a while, he heard movement inside, and then her voice saying, "Who's there?"

"Me, Charlie," he called back, softly.

A fine drizzle was falling, and he stood there outside the shack, cupping his cigarette in his hand, waiting for the key to turn in the lock. The sky was invisible overhead, and all around him was pitch darkness, roughly punctuated by dots of light. The thin wind through the trees made a soft, rasping sound like files rubbing against wood as leaves and branches clashed. He heard the door being unlocked and spun his cigarette away into the dripping night.

Then the door opened partly, and he squeezed through the gap, saying, "Hullo, Freda, girl."

She held a candle in a tin holder, sheltering the flame with a hand until he thrust the door shut again, and locked it.

"Hush," she said. "Don't wake the children." Then, "Out in this rain?"

He joked softly, "What's the matter, you want me to go?"

"Ah, you *full* of nonsense. You stayed away so long, anyhow –"

"*Bokkie, bokkie*," he chuckled, in the trembling candlelight.

Her coarse hair had been done up for the night into

two, short braids on either side of her face, and he could see the heavy mounds of her breasts under the old, floppy, washed-out flannel night-dress she was wearing. He followed her across the room, pulling off his wet slicker, past the children stirring and mumbling on the settee in the front.

He said, "Is nice and warm in here."

"I had the primus burning," she answered. "But it still don't work awright."

Behind the curtain across the room, she said, smiling gently: "Did you come to finish that *dop*?"

"Nah," he grinned. "Drink, hell."

She put the candle down on the old dressing-table by the bed, and his mouth was dry as he watched the movement of her full, round hips under the night-dress.

She asked, mischievously, "Your Ma know you here?"

He smiled, unlacing his muddy boots. "Maybe she guesses. Well, she said I'm a big man, now."

She said, "You never got married, Charlie."

He said, "No. Maybe I was shell-shock in the war." This mention of marriage disturbed him a little, and he joked it away, hoping she would not pursue the subject.

She was close to him, and the candle burned on the dressing-table that was scattered with discarded clothes and other paraphernalia: half-used jars of face-cream, salves, deodorants, a tarnished metal tube of lipstick, a cake of used toilet soap in a saucer, a worn suspender belt: all the accumulated loot filched from madam's boudoir. A ripped nylon stocking hung like a captured standard from a fly-blown wing mirror.

She smiled at him, but the candle was a stage light that cast shadows and picked up only the reflection of her eyes, so that he could not see the smile. But he could see the depth of her eyes and a softness there that took on a beauty he had not noticed before, and then she was struggling a little against his sudden brutality, quivering as he ground himself against her and his hands sang on her body.

"Charlie. Charlie. Charlie, man."

"And you? You? You?"

"Charlie, you so *wild,* man."

But her half-hearted resistance dissolved under his searching, and he heard her deep, contented sighs as he lay crushed into her breasts, feeling her tremble and the harsh tenderness of her rough, charwoman's hands on his face. There was a roaring in his ears and her sighs were now moans as their bodies locked desperately, her mouth soft, tasting faintly of soapiness, and he slid into the pleasure without thought, like a stone into a pool, and was swallowed up in the fierce woman's smell of her armpits and breasts and the enveloping heat of her thighs.

Chapter Fourteen

A strip of asphalt, holed and cracked and scattered with stony pools, straggled for a short length among the shanties, and then was lost in an undergrowth of weeds. It was the corpse of a street that had died a long time ago, choked to death by neglect and left to be nudged and toed by the surrounding hovels which lay on its crumbling flanks like hyenas waiting to devour it.

A few old brick and plaster houses still stood, or rather tottered, at intervals along the ruined street. Most of their windows had gone, and cardboard, box-wood or stuffed rags gave the impression of rough patches over gaping eye-sockets. Paint and plaster had fallen from the walls, leaving raw wounds of brickwork, and roofs were held down with rows of boulders. These houses stood a little aside from the other tin-and-cardboard dwellings with an air of shabby aloofness, like somewhat better-off relatives compelled to associate with the rest of the impoverished family.

Ronny Pauls slouched into the street from between two shanties and paused for a moment by the edge of the crumbling asphalt. A fine drizzle was falling and it had soaked the shoulders of his jacket, and now, facing the drizzle, it began to seep into his shirt. He shivered under the bite of the rain, and tugged at his cap to keep the drizzle out of his eyes.

He crossed the street, walking with his body hunched and his hands deep in the pockets of his trousers. Around him the fine fall of rain hissed, and the leaves of the trees made a quiet, brushing sound, like brooms across rough ground. He reached the other side of the decrepit street and turned down a row of sodden houses. On the edge of the asphalt he stumbled in a pot-hole and cursed, his body flaying to keep its balance. He straightened, slithering through mud and wet leaves.

Ahead of him watery light dribbled through cracks in a boarded-up window. The house had been four-roomed once, long ago, but one side and the back had collapsed, leaving a rambling pile of wet rubble and the gaping interior walls, like the scene of a bombing. All that was left were a front room and the kitchen.

The front garden had been engulfed by a sticky pudding of wet clay and black mud, and Ronald plodded the few steps through it to the cracked and peeling front door, dark and ugly as that of a haunted house in a movie picture. He shivered and dragged a hand from his wet pocket to knock.

Almost fantastically, a gramophone was playing inside, and he heard the music through the splintery panels, a shrill, distorted voice singing something about moonlight and roses and memories. He rapped again, stamping his feet on the single, broken step. Somebody inside shouted through the grinding music, another voice scolded in reply. Then the lock squeaked and rattled and the door was opened about two inches.

"Hey, whatisit?"

From the narrow bar of insipid yellow light a rectangle of face peered out at him: wrinkled brown skin, like crumpled wrapping paper, strands of grey hair and an eye swimming in an egg-cupful of liquid, a serrated crack of a mouth, and, gripping the edge of the door, a hand for all the world like a brown chicken-claw.

"I want to see Susie," Ronny said, his mind cursing the rain and the horrible old woman. "Is she in. Tell her it's Ronny-boy."

"She's not here," the old woman screeched. "Go away. What you come here for Susie for?" Behind her the record whined under a blunt needle.

"I want to see her," Ronald urged. "Tell her –"

"Man, I told you she isn't here. Go away, go away."

Ronald opened his mouth to say something else, but the door was shut in his face, and there was the sound of the lock and the gathering speed of the distorted crooning as the gramophone was wound rapidly. He raised a hand to knock again, but gave up the idea, thinking, What's the use, the old bitch. Hatred unpeeled itself inside him, and beyond the door the voice now started singing metallically, something about Hawaii.

The blerry bastard bitch, she better not mess me around, Ronald was thinking as he turned from the door. She better not bogger around with other *jubas* or I'll give her what for. He stumbled away through the oozing muck and strewn bricks, rage and disappointment mingling with the unravelling knots of hatred.

He crossed the street in the drizzle. Under a dripping gum tree he told himself, I bet you she's inside there, playing that . . . gramophone, waiting for a . . . man. He stood hunched in the cold, one hand holding close the collar of his jacket. Somewhere behind him a dog started up a barking and snarling, flinging itself against a length of chain. Ronald moved instinctively away, not thinking of the dog, and waited on the edge of the crumbling street.

After a while he decided to light a cigarette and drew one gingerly from a crushed packet, lighting it carefully in his cupped hands. But in a few minutes it had dissolved into a hairy brown mess in the rain, and he flung the ruins bitterly into the mud. He stood there, watching the house, his mind wriggling with anger, and his damp fingers touched the two-and-sixpenny jack-knife in his pocket. Rain soaked through his clothes and he sneezed, wiped his upper lip with the edge of a wet finger. He was still thinking painfully of the girl, Susie, when he saw the bulky figure slosh up the broken street and stop in front of the house. The man wore an old overcoat and he bobbed up and down to warm himself, on the doorstep. After a few moments the door was opened and the gramophone music came again, mockingly, into the dripping darkness. The man said something to the old woman at the door and she held it wide and he pushed inside.

There was a loose floorboard in the front room, and it creaked when walked upon. The floor itself was muddy and bore the remains of a linoleum cover which now looked like the peeling scab of a great sore. The room was cramped with battered and warped furniture moved into it when the rest of the house had collapsed, and the ceiling boards were buckled, stuffed with newspapers where they gaped. There were big patches of damp all over and the distemper was flaking from the walls or bulging in great wet blisters.

The old crone crossed the room towards the kitchen, crying in her screeching voice: "Always blerry men. If it not one is the other one. Just staying with men, men, men." She wore a long, filthy dress that reached to her ankles and a pair of tattered slippers slap-slapped across the floor as she walked, one of them revealing the nail of a big toe, yellow and cracked and dirty, like a relic unearthed from a tomb.

The girl, Susie Meyer, who was winding the gramophone on a table by the large, unmade bed, snapped at her:

"Shut up! Stop your mouth! Is it your blerry business?"

Roman laughed as he struggled out of the old khaki greatcoat he was wearing. Some of the buttons were missing and the shoulder-straps dangled loose. The coat was dark with rain.

The girl moved the arm of the gramophone onto the record and the crooner's distorted voice whined out of the big horn. She sat on the edge of the soiled bed and listened.

Roman said, "Tell the *ou* lady to bring a dop. Is damn' cold."

"You go tell her," Susie said. "You see I'm listening."

"Awright." He came towards her grinning. His rotten teeth showed through the stubble over the loose, bloated, rough-skinned face. "Records again?"

"Keep quiet, man. I want to listen."

"Records," he said with a sneer and went over to the kitchen door, to ask the crone for a bottle of cheap wine.

The girl sat on the bed, her face wrapt, listening to the nasal voice. It was a crudely pretty face, the cheekbones brightened with rouge, and the lashes too heavy with mascara, the heavy mouth smeared with glaring lipstick that didn't match her complexion, and the wiry hair held in a number of plastic curlers gave her a ludicrous golliwog appearance. She sat there, absorbing the scratchy sounds of love and moonlight.

The record was hissing to an end when Roman came in again, holding a bottle. He said, "How goes it, Susie?"

"I bought me some new Bings," the girl said, starting to crank the machine. "I wish we had lectrick and a wi'less."

Roman put the neck of the bottle to his mouth, tipped his head back and drank. Some of the orange-yellow wine ran down his chin from a corner of his mouth. He took the bottle away and belched loudly. "Where you get chink for records. Jesus, here I am without a penny for a decent *dop*."

"What's it got to do with you, hey?" she frowned at him. "Is you my husband?" Then she changed her tone and said, "Two lates' Bings. I was going to buy a Frankie Lane, but it wasn't such a nice song."

Roman swallowed some more wine and then asked, watching her: "Listen, what about that lighty, Ronny Pauls?"

"What about him?" She tilted the curling-pinned head at him, smiling with narrowed, painted eyes.

"Hell, you leave the blerry lighties alone."

She laughed, a shrill, unnerving sound, something like a cross between a crow and a jangle, and then sneered: "Look here, I can go out with anybody I want to, don't I say? If you so partickler, stay by your house with your wife and children."

"Don't talk crack," Roman said, and took another drink. He hated being reminded of his wife and children. It was cold and uncomfortable in the awful room, but it was better than he was used to. He leaned against a sagging sideboard, feeling drunk. His puffed, blood-shot eyes stared back at him from the brown-stained mirror.

The girl said, tauntingly, "I hear that Charlie Pauls pulled you up nice."

Roman glared at her. "Him? Me? Pull *me* up?"

"*Ja.* You got marks on your face, too."

"Eff him," Roman said, sullenly. "I'll get him again. And I'll break that other lighty's blerry neck."

The girl laughed again. She picked up a cigarette from beside the gramophone and lighted it, blowing smoke and smiling at the bullet-headed ruin standing against the old sideboard. Outside, the drizzle hissed. Then she started to wind the gramophone again.

Roman said, "Can't you leave that thing alone? Let's talk a little, hey?"

"I know what *you* want to talk," she said. "How much you got?" But he did not reply, and she slid a record from its sleeve onto the turn-table and the needle whispered in the groove until the music came. "Bing is real wake-up. I saw one of his pieces four times."

Roman scowled at her, while she sat entranced as the voice wailed from the horn, distorted by old springs, blunt needle and a damaged amplifier.

"Real wake-up," the girl sighed. "But I wish we had a wi'less."

Chapter Fifteen

Roman lived with his family in what looked like an amalgamation of a kennel, a chicken-coop and a lean-to shed. A wretched affair, even its meanness looked dilapidated. Within it, he, his wife and eleven children crowded like rabbits in a hutch whenever shelter was necessary. When it was not, the children wandered about clad in a dirty vest, or an old shirt, a torn jersey and nothing else. They were pot-bellied with hunger and scratched around like chickens wherever they found themselves, searching for discarded titbits: a mouldy crust, a gnawed bone, a sticky condensed milk tin. The mother sat in the doorway looking withered as a branch of a blasted tree.

A common labourer, Roman had drifted from one mean job to another, earning a few shillings here, a few shillings there. Finally, despairing, perhaps, about the upkeep of his offspring, he took to petty thieving, robbing the weaker ones around him. Now and then he robbed out of bounds, and found himself in jail.

Between terms of imprisonment, he took to drinking and blamed all his miseries on his wife. Having no capacity for any sort of advanced thought, he struck at those nearest to himself, and he went for them like a drowning man clawing madly over the heads of other drowning shipwrecks, in order to reach the dubious safety of a drifting oar.

He bought cheap wine with whatever money he

managed to cajole, steal and sometimes earn. When he could not afford even the cheapest wine, he got drunk on a sixpenny-worth of methylated spirits.

When he was home, all who lived near them could hear the sounds of Roman's brutality. He beat his wife's head with faggots, or her face with his fists. He kicked her ribs and broke her arms. When he became tired of beating her, he whipped the children. Most of the time he was in a state of drunken savagery, and when he had no wine, or the means of procuring any, he was as dangerous as a starved old wolf, ready to turn on anybody who got in his way.

Once his wife had been more or less good-looking. But Roman had knocked her teeth to stumps and her face to a bundle of scar-tissue. Whatever love she might have borne him, turned ultimately to hatred, and at times she had fought back. But after a few years of beatings and wretched living, even hatred had dried up, leaving her like a rag doll, torn and savaged by a mongrel who had finally pawed the sawdust out of it and was left only with a few scraps of dirty ribbons. Her resistance gone, their fighting became no longer a spectacle to be enjoyed by the neighbours, and so Roman's violence was accepted as a matter of course, and they were left to fight in peace.

Miraculously, life clung on in the woman's womb. There seemed never a time when she was not about to have a child or had just been delivered of one. This appalled and enraged Roman even further. His wife became with child as regularly as clock-work. She gave birth as smoothly as a grease-gun gives grease: you simply push the plunger and the grease comes out. So that above his raving, there was always the screams of children.

He turned to some of the loose women in the settlement in order to avoid his wife. But when he was rejected by them because of his wretchedness and poverty, he returned home and attacked his wife. The morning Charlie Pauls had whipped him, Roman went back to his hovel and bludgeoned her, as a sort of compensation for his own defeat.

Nobody knew where it would end. Few cared, they had troubles of their own.

Chapter Sixteen

The drizzle had stopped; everywhere there was water, stagnant lakes spreading among the dripping shanties, and the tracks had become black pools joined like beads by untidy threads of wetness, and the leaves of port-jackson and gum trees tap-tap-tapped their moisture in a wintry morse onto the sodden rooftops. People made their way from track to track, skipping across the puddles, or plodded through the sticky mud. Children waded happily, and sailed flotillas of wood-chips across the brown lakes, and from doorways little cataracts spilled into the sandlots as flooded shacks were baled out. Everywhere was the smell of rain, mixed with the general smell of the settlement, fused into a pervading perfume of bitter dereliction.

When Charlie entered the Pauls yard, he knew immediately that something was wrong. There was an atmosphere of gloom that had nothing to do with the weather, and what was more, Alfie and Ronald hung about the yard when they should have been off to work long ago. On the kitchen step, Caroline stood, big and heavy, her blotched, doll-face straining with trapped emotion.

"What's the matter?" Charlie asked. "You boggers not working today?"

Alfred looked at him with an expression full of bewilderment and gloom; and Ronald said, with sharp directness: "Is Darra. He died just now." He turned away with a scowl and thrust his hands into the pockets of his trousers.

Charlie gaped at them, looking from one to the other, and then sighed, "No. No, man." He lunged towards the house and thrust past Caroline whose swollen face burst suddenly into an ugly explosion of tears. In the kitchen Charlie could hear the boy, Jorny, weeping in their room, and from behind the shabby curtain over the doorway to the parents' room came a strange, harsh chant.

It was Ma. She sat in the straight-backed chair by the bed, her hands folded in her lap, and her body rocked gently back and forth as she half-sang and half-spoke. The words came flat and parchment-dry from under the black headcloth, while her back rocked slowly, her eyes staring at the wall in front of her.

Charlie said, "Ma–"

"Your Darra's gone away," Ma intoned. "Your pa's gone away and he not coming back no more. Your pa was a good man to me, and he worked all the time so we could eat, and he gave me his children and he saw them grow up. He was a good man to me and to his children, and he trusted in Our Lord. He just lived and worked and didn't do nothing that was wrong in the eyes of the Lord. He worked for his family and when he couldn't work no more, he lay down and waited for the Lord Jesus to take him away. Now he's gone away to the Lord and he's away from sickness and hunger and gone to rest from his work. He carried his cross, too, like Our Lord Jesus, and now the burden is taken from off his shoulders . . . ."

The harsh, tearless voice chanted on and the shoulders rocked. There were no tears in Ma Pauls, but her words were her tears.

Charlie stared at the bed, and felt his throat clog. Dad Pauls lay quiet now under the straightened, unravelling blanket, and his face stared up from the soiled pillows, charred with stubble and blank as a mask, while Ma's words dropped around him.

Charlie said, again, "Ma–"

Then the quiet chanting ceased and the rocking frame grew still. Ma sat silently for a few moments, and then the reins of government were gathered again, and she spoke to Charlie.

"Your poor pa got to be washed down, Charles," she said. "You send Jorny-boy with a bucket and tell him to bring some water. There's a tickey on the shelf in the kitchen."

"Okay, Ma," Charlie answered, quietly.

"Then you send Ronny up to the doctor. He got to give a certificate, *mos*, isn't it? On the way he can tell Mister Sampie what colleck the burial money every week. Your pa's burial booky is paid up. I'm glad we managed that."

"Right, Ma."

She sighed and went on. "You better go and call Missus Nzuba to give a hand. She'd want to he'p. She he'ped with Ca'line's wedding, and she'll be cross if I don't ask her to he'p. Then go tell Brother Bombata and your Uncle Ben, and other people. People got to be told, I reckon."

"Okay, Ma," Charlie said, moving to the door. He hesitated, then added a little gruffly: "Ma, don't you go taking on, hey?"

"I's awright," Ma said, not looking at him. "I better go see Ca'line lies down. I don't want her opset at this time."

When Charlie was gone, she arose and went to the

chest of drawers and rummaged in it, until she found an old cardboard chocolate-box. It was full of worn and tattered papers: marriage lines, birth certificates, receipts, the children's Sunday-school cards, all the records of a family's life. She took out the burial-insurance book with Dad Pauls' name on it, and put the rest of the papers away. She opened a frayed purse and extracted two pennies. Then, leaning over the bed, placed a coin on each of Dad Pauls' eyes. His hands were folded under the blanket. Then Ma went to the battered wardrobe to find a clean shirt.

In the kitchen, Caroline was sobbing quietly, and Ma said to her: "How you feeling, my child?"

"Awright, I think, Ma," Caroline said, wrackingly. She wiped her face and left a grimy smear on each cheek.

Ma said, "Now you go and lie down, and tell Alfy to sit by you. There's nothing for you children to do now. Will Alfy lose a day if he don't go to work?"

"Don't know, Ma."

"Awright. Go lie down, now. I got to fix the fire."

Outside, the sky maintained its steely look, and the trees were wet. Somewhere voices shouted in conversation across fences, and dogs broke into an uproar of barking. In the street beyond the house, a horse-drawn cart went by, lurching and bumping through the muddy ruts and rain-filled holes, its wheels sneding up little fountains of water as it passed. The cart was laden with firewood covered with scraps of wet sacking, and a barefoot boy walked behind it to watch for faggots which might fall from the pile. An old man sat on top of the load, hunched in the cold, his whiskery face as gaunt as a prophet's, and every few moments he flicked at the nag's back with a switch. The cart bounced along

109

the lane, and one of its wheels made a high, shrill, tortured sound.

Footsteps splashed in the yard, and a figure appeared in the kitchen doorway, its face agitated and tearful. The whole house creaked and sagged as this woman entered.

Ma said, looking up from the stove, "Morning, Nzuba."

Given: a huge black currant jelly that had been moulded into a series of connected ovals, spheres, elipses and sundry bulges representing head, torso, arms and legs. Attire this jelly in a vast dress, washed out and then once more soiled with grease and spilled food; pull over the dress a man's coat, old and bursting at the seams, and refusing to button in front; a man's stretched, darned and holed socks over the elephantine calves, and a man's cracked and shapeless, cast-off shoes on the great feet. Result: Missus Nzuba.

Her mouth, when she spoke or smiled, became a swelling and contracting bubble on a boiling sphere of chocolate blancmange. Whenever she moved, even if only a little finger, the whole vast mound of her body shook and bounced and quivered as if a million slack little springs had been set into action beneath the undulating expanse of her skin.

Now, seeing Ma Pauls, she cried, "Ai, Pauls, Charlie just came to tell me. Ai, shame. I'm so sorry, Pauls. Shame, shame, shame."

"*Dankie*, thanks, is awright, Nzuba," Ma told her, gently. "I'm glad you can give a little he'p here."

"We got to yelp each other. Shame," the other woman said, and wiped away a tear with the edge of her coat. She asked: "Was it very bad, Pauls?"

"No," Ma told her, poking at the fire. "He went

quiet. I was just sitting there by him, after he had some soup from last night. Then he look at me and he say, 'Rachy,' – he always called me Rachy, *mos*, you know – 'Rachy,' he say, 'is the children awright?' And I say, '*Ja*, Dad, the children is awright. Why do you worry?' And he say, again, 'I would have like them to be living in another place. Like thos houses with tile roofs.' And, '*Ach*, what,' I say. 'You never min' about the house,' I say. And he just look at me and close his eyes. Then he give a sort of sigh and then the next thing, there's the rattle in his throat, and he pass away just like that." Ma was silent for a while, recollecting the moment, and Missus Nzuba wiped her eyes.

"Well, Pauls," she said, sniffing as if she had a cold. "You *darem* got your children by you."

"*Ja,* the children," Ma sighed. "The children. But I don't know, Nzuba. Is like there's something happening with the family. But maybe is in all families, hey. Jorny-boy don't want to go to school no more, always turning sticks, playing truant. Scratching around the rubbish tip with other children whole day. And Ronny is getting wilder and wilder, I reckon, and I don't know what Charles is going to do."

"How," Missus Nzuba said, with commiseration. "The children of today."

Then Ma said, "I sent Jorny for water. You can he'p me wash the old man, and things. I hope Jorny don't stay long."

"You can have some water by my house," Missus Nzuba said. "Is hot awready. Then we don't have to wait, hey. Is there somebody to send?"

"I'll let you have it back," Ma told her. "We can send Alfy."

"I don't want it back, man," the other woman said.

"I'm proud to yelp you. We been living here together a long time."

Ma said, "*Dankbaar*, Nzuba. I'm thankful to you."

"There's no need to be thankful. We all got to stand by each other. Is Alfred there? I'll send him for the water by my house."

Chapter Seventeen

There is water in the threatening sky, and water in the healthy earth; water in copper pipes and iron cisterns. Water to boil coffee, or to wash scraps of clothes. Water with which to wash the dead. Water is precious, and in the yards of those whose sand-lots had been laid with plumbing, the queues of scarecrow children form up with buckets and cans and saucepans. Those who owned the plumbing and the taps sold the water to those who lacked such amenities. Because a man's got to live, hasn't he?

"Mister, my ma say a bucket of water till Friday."

"Friday? Friday? Wait till Friday for tuppence? Your ma must be *bedonerd*, crazy. Tuppence a bucket, cash."

"My ma haven't got tuppence now, *mos*, mister."

"Is that *my* fault? Go on, go on. I haven't got time to blerry-well waste."

"Hey, you bastard, I came here first. Don't I say?"

"*Garn*. I was standing here first, all the time."

". . . you. I was standing here. Ask her. Wasn't I standing here?"

"Listen, you little boggers, if you can't blerry-well behave, you'll get bogger-all, see?"

"Missus, my ma say a tin of water till Friday."

"Barnshoot! No pay, no water. Friday."

"I say, you reckon you can get a blerry bathful of blerry water for a twopence? What the hell you think this is, a sale?"

"Well, is *mos* tuppence whatever you bring, don't I say?"

"Listen, you dirty-nose, don't be cheeky with me. I'll kick your blerry backside, understand?"

"Well, a tin's a tin. You never said what size."

"Smart lighty, hey? Bring a blerry bath and reckon you going to get it full?"

"Mister, the can's not full to the top. You got to make it full to the top."

"Awright, awright, hold your hair. There."

Water gurgling, splashing, drumming into buckets, cans, jugs, pots. Water with which to brew the morning coffee, with which to wash pa's Sunday shirt. Sometimes you even use it to wash yourself. Water with which to wash the new-born babe, or the dead.

Water is profit. In order to make this profit, the one who sells the water must also use it to wash his soul clean of compassion. He must rinse his heart of pity, and with the bristles of enterprise, scrub his being sterile of sympathy. He must have the heart of a stop-cock and the brain of a cistern, intestines of lead pipes.

"Mister, half a bucket. We only got a penny."

"Half-a-bucket? Half-a-bucket. Jesus Christ in heaven, what the hell must a man do with a penny?"

"My ma say a tinful of water till tomorrow, mister. True as God, mister, till tomorrow."

"Tell your ma I say tomorrow never come. Tomorrow. What you think I am – a blerry millionaire?"

"*Howkees*, this is a stingy man, hey."

"Stingy? Stingy. With whom do you think you are talking? Stingy."

"*Ou* pal, give the lighties some water till Friday, man."

"Look, *ou pal*, who's stuffing this cow? Me or you?

114

Till Friday. Till tomorrow. God on earth, if they don't pay *now*, I'll never get the blerry money."

"Hell, don't be like that, mister."

"Hey, man, this is my blerry place. Blow, man."

"Gwan, you reckon you strong, hey? I was standing here first."

"No fighting, no fighting."

"Gwan, you come out ape."

"Jussus, we all poor people."

"Me, I'm poor also. What you reckon I eat? Stones? Grass?"

"Mister, a bucket of water."

"One tin of water, mister."

"Say, please. Haven't you got no blerry manners?"

Chapter Eighteen

Now the house was crowded with mourners, and in the yard those who could not get in stood around under the gnarled mulberry in the damp sand, and listened to the hymn-singing inside. Most of the men had put on their Sunday best, black suits lifted down from wardrobes and brushed, or shiny navy-blue wear, and black ties. The women wore hats, most of them, like the men's suits, kept for the special occasion of a wedding or a funeral. The black or blue suits seemed to embarrass those who wore work-a-day clothes, and these moved a little shyly in the crowd. Relations and neighbours were assembled there, swarthy mulatto faces and very dark African, all looking solemn, for there is unity even in death.

Charlie stood in the yard and shook hands with those who arrived. His dark suit, purchased a long time ago, had grown tight around the shoulders and too short at the ankles, and he was secretly wishing that the whole business was over so that he could shed the clothes. Nearby, Ronald, looking more sullen than sad, also accepted the formal commiserations of the arrivals.

"Deepest sympathy, my boy."

"The Lord knows best."

"Look nice after your ma, hey?"

"Be brave, my boy."

Charlie smiled and nodded, and ushered people towards the house.

Most of the crowd inside were women, who had been given the privilege of viewing the corpse. The men smoked and murmured in the grey daylight, outside. Now and then there was a small press around the kitchen door when somebody became determined to get inside to do his duty to the widow. Inside women were singing shrilly and discordantly. In the yard, others hushed the children who scampered around like terriers.

The wind roared slowly through the trees and faces turned anxiously towards the battle-grey sky.

Charlie saw Freda and his face broke into a smile. The solemnity of the occasion seemed to have turned everybody around him into strangers, as if death had stripped friends of happiness and disguised them with the shrouds of sorrow. But seeing the woman, he felt the warmth for her come to life, and he said, moving across: "Hell, Freda, I reckoned you was working today."

"I asked the missus the afternoon off. I would have taken it, anyway."

"You want to go inside?"

"Don't worry, man. I'll see the old lady afterwards." The dark, handsome face was soft under the hat of three fashions ago, cast off by madam. She smiled at others around her.

"Good day, sister," Uncle Ben said, and tried to bow with formality with his waistcoated paunch. "A sad time, a sad time."

He had had a few surreptitious drinks before coming, and his normally woeful eyes seemed to be drowning in puddles of despair.

Charlie said, quietly, "I wish this was all over." He watched the sky and then frowned about him.

"Charlie," Freda admonished, softly. "And your own pa, too."

"Ah, I can't he'p it," Charlie told her. He smiled slyly at her, happier now that she was near him. "Okay if I come around again, tonight?"

"Hush. You should not be talking like that now, man."

"Ah, Freda, Freda."

"Look, the people is coming out."

The crowd from inside was spilling out into the yard now. Charlie said to Freda, "You wait here, hey. Don't walk away."

He signalled to Ronny and Alfred to follow him into the house. He, Ronny, Alfred and Uncle Ben were the chief pallbearers, and when they came out again, they were carrying the coffin, working it out of the cramped house, assisted by two other men. According to the subscriptions Dad Pauls had paid, it would be a twenty-pound funeral, Mister Sampie, the undertaker's agent had told them. A hearse, and a car for the family, and of course, the coffin.

"With his name on it," Ma had said, softly. "Dad would like a nice coffin with silver handles and his name cut out on a silver plate."

So there was the coffin with its shiny fittings, and the crowd shuffling behind it, many carrying wreaths and bunches of flowers. Some of the women cried, but Ma was dry and grim under her black headcloth and widow's weeds. The mourners filled the little back street with its muddy ruts and the frowning grey canopy of sky over it. Then the coffin rolled into the hearse and piled with flowers. The driver of the big, black car held the door open.

"You sit in the back, Ma," Charlie said. "Ca'line and

118

Jorny-boy can sit with you. Is Missus Nzuba going, too?"

"No," Ma said, inside the car. "She said she'll stay and look after the house."

"Good job, too," Charlie mumbled. "That *ou* lady need a car all by herself. Ca'line's big enough in here."

"Shhh," Ma told him. "Is no time for your jokes."

Caroline and Jorny were in the car. They were both crying, and the girl looked ugly and awkward.

"Let Uncle Ben sit in front," Ma said. "What about you?"

"I'll walk with the other friends," Charlie replied.

"I'll walk, too," Uncle Ben said. "Us men'll walk. Is okay."

"There's place," Ma said. "Let Freda sit in front, then. Tell her."

And Charlie warmed at this, feeling that it meant that Freda was being accepted. He smiled at her, helping her in, and when she was on the front seat, he winked at her but she was looking straight ahead, preserving the decorum of the occasion.

The driver said, "Mind your fingers," and slammed the door.

The hearse moved ahead, heaving slowly on the muddy surface of the lane, and the car lumbered after it. Charlie and the other men of the family took up their places behind the car and the rest of the mourners fell in behind them. The sky was one immense, untidy sweep of heavy cloud.

The cortège crawled slowly among the ramshackle cabins, past the silent watchers on the flanks, and gained the ruined street that would take it into the suburb. The feet of the procession crunched on broken, but hard surface, now, making crackling sounds.

119

Up ahead, in front of the hearse, walked Mister Sampie, the undertaker's agent. He was a small, brown, knobbly man, like a peanut. Off duty he was chirpy, but now he had assumed the guise of an attendant upon death, and he plodded along at the correct pace, with an air of sadness, hands clasped professionally behind his back; and he carried a sort of distorted pride in the pair of baggy striped trousers and an old, pressed swallow-tailed coat which constituted his uniform.

And beside him walked Brother Bombata. Woolly-haired, and black as a beetle, he trudged ahead with his own professional air, clutching a dog-eared Bible against his side; and with his flaring nostrils and long, gloomy face, looking for all the world like an aging horse in a white celluloid collar.

Through the streets of the suburb the procession moved.

Faces watched over the garden walls and fences. A man on a sidewalk removed his hat and stood at attention until the hearse had passed him. The sky was unpleasant as death itself, and a few scattered drops began to fall. By the time the cortège reached the cemetery it was drizzling again, finely.

Charlie was hoping that the burial would be a quick one, so that they wouldn't get caught in a heavy shower. So he was a little irritated when Brother Bombata launched into a long, droning sermon while the crowd huddled around the open grave, among the tombstones, withered flowers, broken jam-jars, the neglected mounds and in-loving-memories and never-to-be-for-gottens.

A finch descended, crying shrilly, from the sky and came to rest on a branch near the grave. It watched for a moment, its head cocked, and then suddenly fluttered and started away, flying like an arrow between the trees.

Brother Bombata went on, his deep, sad, professional voice rising and falling through the clash of branches moved by the wind. And then at last, it was time for the coffin to be lowered and the grave to be filled. Some of the women wept a little; and Freda wiped away tears from the corners of her eyes, and Caroline cried in harsh, hacking sounds.

Only Ma did not cry. She stood stolidly at the head of the grave while Charlie, Alfred, Ronald and Uncle Ben shovelled the first sand into the hole.

Charlie worked quickly and expertly. He was used to working with a shovel, and he drove the blade into the soil with determination, as if he was digging ditches again, and the spades of earth flew into the grave, dropping with regular thuds onto the coffin. Alfred worked with care, dropping in small heaps, working as if he was being forced to commit sacrilege and was doing so with apologies. Ronald shovelled the earth in sullenly, his mind somewhere else, ignoring the damp thudding as the bright metal engraving of Dad Pauls's name and date of birth and death was covered up. Uncle Ben panted and wheezed as he handled his shovel. Liquor had shortened his breath, and he hoped desperately that somebody would relieve him. The handle was clumsy in his hands, and the blade jerked dangerously, ready to gash a leg that happened into its way. So he was glad, his breath sobbing with relief, when Charlie straightened up and signalled them to pass the tools over to others who waited.

The grave was filled and people sang, and under the black headcloth Ma's face looked hard and drawn, the small, wrinkled mouth tight as a sewn-up wound, the eyes like scraps of charred cloth. Only her shoulders were bowed, a little more than usual it seemed, as if she had been given another burden to carry. Around her voices sang discordantly from damp hymn-books, "Abide with me, soft falls the eventide . . ." while the grave was banked with flowers.

Chapter Nineteen

But there is a time for laughter and for merriment. Jannie Fransman can play the guitar. His hands, normally like iron grabs, are now as delicate as a surgeon's, and his long fingers dance over the frets and strings, making the music boom and tinkle in the smoky room. The fire is glowing happily in the big iron brazier, and Aunt Mina has brought out the eight-gallon drum of corn beer. Aunt Mina is stout, with a face plump and brown, glossy as well-polished leather. Jannie Fransman's fingers stroke and pluck the strings, fast, slow, combinations of notes, long runs twanging against the ear. "'Merican chords," murmur the onlookers and the listeners. The fire is bright and it is warm in the crowded room, and the corn beer is selling fast. So somebody wants to sing. Girls lean on the furniture, chins on hands, waiting for the songs.

"Play a sentimental, Jannie."

"Play something sad."

There is a young boy who belongs to the coon bands, the New Year minstrel shows, and he can sing "Danny Boy" with all the emotion, so it brings a lump into the throat. Or he can chant the slave-songs, handed down over three hundred years from chattels and Dutch sailors: *"Onder deze piesang boompie, al op een eilandtje...."*

"Listen, Smallboy, sing us a Western, man."

And the old guitar, scarred like a veteran, hums and

123

throbs the sounds from the plains thousands of miles away: "Oh, bury me not on the lone prairie", or "The yellow rose of Texas". And as the night moves on, there would be a sadness in everybody, and all would sing together, "Memories" and "Mother", and "I'll take you home again, Kathleen".

Perhaps there would be one of the African customers who had brought along his concertina, and everybody would join the shaking, shuffling dance to the jigging wail of keys and bellows.

"Hear me, I got one-and-four left. You reckon we could come together for another roun'?"

"Can work, pally. Maybe Aunty will give us something on the book till next Friday."

Between the songs there are stories to tell, jokes to pass on. "Now wait a minute, I got a joke. You *jubas* hear this one? If the ladies won't min', hey. Is about a Englishman, a Irishman, Scotchman and a Jew. . . ."

Long after midnight it is all over. The company has dwindled tiredly. The last few hangers-on stay a while, yawning, moist-eyed, and the guitar has sunk to a gentle strumming, soft as the drifting smoke.

Chapter Twenty

The night was blank and cold again, and the clouds heavy and pregnant with rain, like a woman waiting her time. In the small room over the garage, George Mostert paced restlessly across the greasy floor, and wondered whether he should take the plunge and accept Charlie Pauls's invitation. Loneliness fought with pride within him, and his teeth gnawed at bitter lips below the tobacco-ginger moustache. Loneliness lurked in the soiled bedding on the scratched wooden bedstead, and the woman's dressing-table that was now cluttered with frayed neckties and discarded socks. Where once there had been talcum dust and spilled lavender-water, tiny barricades of hairpins and grey loops of elastic garters, there were now sticky patterns of teacup rings and an empty brandy bottle.

The scent of powder in the pillows had been replaced by the smell of motor oil and alcohol; the cries of connubial bliss had given way to nagging thoughts of self-pity.

George Mostert stopped at the window and peered out into the chill darkness. A car swept by, roaring into the north. Beyond the scanty undergrowth along the road was life. Why, he thought, a man might have a good time down there, even in all that muck. But a warped sense of loftiness jabbed him with the painful ice-pick of doubt, making him think, Maybe it ain't right, people like us should mix with them. After all. . . .

Some time after midnight it was raining again. This time it was a curtain of grey beads drawn down over the night, a steady, swift fall, rattling on roofs and bouncing high from the surface of roads. The rain was grey and blank, but it possessed a certain personality, a cutting, muttering, gurgling, sucking, bubbling personality, like a homicidal imbecile with a knife.

The line of police cars, trucks and riot vans moved through the streets of the suburb, under the rain, their headlamps making yellow patches in the black-grey darkness. Inside the convoy the men sat stolidly, listening to the hiss and rattle on the canopies of the vehicles. Some of them turned up the collars of their mackintoshes and rubber ponchos, as if they felt the iciness trickling down their necks. The tyres buzzed and swished on the asphalt, and when they lurched across the faults in the streets, the men bounced up and down, but still sitting with stolid faces, listening to the rain. There was little conversation among them.

At the end of the suburb, the convoy split up, breaking in two, each part swinging away from the other in a pincer movement. Now the mud began, and the wheels slewed and skidded a little, and the drivers nursed the steering, peeping out through the wire-meshed windshields towards the yellow, liquid light ahead.

A man climbed out onto the running-board of each of the leading cars, cursing as the rain caught him, hanging onto the wet metal of the bodywork, while he watched ahead and called directions to the driver. The cars and trucks lurched and heaved and staggered forward, then finally they stopped and the settlement was flanked by lines of vehicles.

Officers and sergeants called orders and men began

to clamber out into the rain, and the rain stained the khaki mackintoshes and gleamed quickly on the rubber ponchos. There were police wearing pistol harness outside their raincoats, and African and Coloured constables huddled in ponchos and khaki topis, carrying long riot staves, all in the rain, their polished boots gathering mud. Soon afterwards they moved in groups towards the houses. There were lights burning in some of the shacks, dull yellow, like brass buttons on wet serge.

George Mostert had left it too late. He had finally made up his mind to visit the township, taking the plunge at last, just as a man is forced to jump from a cliff-top in front of a herd of stampeding cattle. But hesitation had attacked him again, as soon as he found himself on the broken parody of a street that cut raggedly through one end of the jumble of shanties. So he stood in the clammy darkness, trying to convince himself that it was worthwhile, after all.

There were sounds around him, coming out of the darkness. The creek-creek of a cricket, and somewhere far off, the scolding of a dog. He was aware of a stench, too: an all-pervading smell of decaying offal, rotting wood and latrines. It was the smell of abject poverty, just as the scent of two-guineas-an-ounce perfume was the smell of wealth.

And then the rain started, and dissolved what little courage he had kept screwed up in the flimsy scrap of his will. He had brought a bottle half-full of brandy with him, stuffed into the pocket of his raincoat, as a sort of gesture of fellowship, but now he suddenly decided to return to his garage and finish it himself. He preferrred to go back and risk the sharp hooves of loneliness.

So, turning back, with the rain just starting to fall, he almost collided with the girl who had come up in the dark towards him. He caught a whiff of cheap liquor and cheap perfume above the tattered, unkempt rag of his moustache, and shied away like a nervous horse.

"*Hoit*, man," the girl, Susie Meyer, said cheerfully. "What you doing all in the dark, hey?"

"Go away," George Mostert muttered, and started along the ruined street towards the main road. He tried to move around her, but she was there, bobbing with the persistence of a terrier bitch, and the brandy bottle in his raincoat pocket bumped her hip.

"Hey," she cried, falling in step beside him, "What you got there, hey?" She laughed happily. "Got a little *doppie* for us?"

The drizzle fell on them in big drops, and George Mostert stumbled in a pot-hole, but the girl was there, holding onto a sleeve. She peered into the clawed, bitter face, and cried, "Hi, is Mister Mostert, don't I say?" She laughed and held onto his raincoat with her predatory hand.

"Listen, go away you," George Mostert said, sullenly, but a tiny ember of sex was suddenly fanned into life inside him, and its scorch frightened him. She was a woman, probably easy to get with a drink and a few shillings, but he was afraid of the association. One didn't go with coloured girls; it was against the law, anyway.

"Ah, I'll come home with you," Susie Meyer told him. "We'll have a little *dring*, *mos*. It isn't so far to your ga-rarge."

But he said, hurrying on, "No, no."

"*Ach*, man, don't be like that. Listen, we can have a nice time, *mos*."

They reached the muddy slope to the road and George Mostert climbed it hurriedly, with the girl clinging to his sleeve. He did not even have the courage to push her off.

He said, weakly: "I don't want anything to do with you, hey."

"*Garn,*" she smiled through the quickening rain. "You scared? You *mos* a man, don't I say? A man, *mos.*"

"No, no, no."

"You's a funny guy, Mister Mostert. I seen you roun' your ga-rarge. I reckon to myself, that's *mos* a man I like. A wake-up *juba.* A class boy, I reckon. Got money, motor-car." They crossed the road, George Mostert staring ahead. "Listen," Susie Meyer cried. "You got a radio? Records? I like Bing, *mos.* We can listen while we have a drink."

He stopped in the single pallid light under the canopy of the garage and said angrily, "Go away, you hear?" His moustache was damp, and had the appearance of a piece of unravelling wet rope.

But she was as unshakeable as a leech. "Ah, come on, man. We can have a wake-up time."

A smeared mouth smiled up at him, showing a gap in her upper gum, flanked by small, yellow canines, like the fangs of a puppy. The wiry, curled hair was covered by a bright kerchief, knotted under the chin and going limp from the rain. George Mostert thought, She doesn't look so bad. It was the cheap, artificial good looks such as those of a dummy in a shop window; but the treacherous thought said, Not too bad.

The rain fell faster beyond the dim light under the canopy, and he smelled again the cheap perfume and the stale muscadel of her breath. Breathing into his face, she blew out the tiny flame of passion that had flickered inside him, and he pushed her away and scrabbled at the keyhole of the door that led to his room upstairs.

She waited expectantly, smiling with the crudely lacquered, gap-toothed mouth, but he burst suddenly through the doorway and slammed it in her face, leaving the smile to fade away like a once-gaudy pattern on cheap material.

"Ghod," she said to herself. "That blerry *ou* fool. To hell with him." Then she sneered and shrugged, turning away once more towards the rain and the roadway.

Chapter Twenty-One

Police Constable Van Den Woud signalled to two African policemen to follow him and the three of them went through the swamped door-yard of a sagging cabin, their boots sucking and belching in the mud. The rain was icy, needling, and they were all a little angry at having been called out for this raid in such weather. The two Africans wore the usual ponchos and carried riot staves, long, slender clubs with oval heads. Van Den Woud wore his gun-harness outside his raincoat, the holster buttoned to keep the water out. In any case, he did not expect trouble.

The house was in darkness, and Van Den Woud ordered one of his men to knock. The man stepped forward in the mud and banged on the door. The whole house seemed to shudder. All over, little squads were banging on doors and shouting. Lights were being lit where shanties had been in darkness, and there was a babble of voices forming an undertone to the rain.

The man banged on the door again, and Van Den Woud shouted, "Come on, open up. Open the ... door."

After a few moments he thrust the African policemen aside and, stepping back a pace, raised his booted foot and drove it at the lock. The shanty trembled and shook and somebody started shouting inside. A light flickered on beyond the patched window, and at the same moment the lock burst and the door flew open.

Constable Van Den Woud lurched into the tiny, stale,

smoky room, carried forward by his own momentum, and came to a halt, cursing. The others crowded in behind him. A naked African stood holding a lamp in one hand, and covering his privates with the other. He stood, a dark, posed statue. Beyond him, in a rumpled bed, a woman's face stared frightenedly over the blankets drawn up to her chin.

"Alright, alright," Constable Van Den Woud started shouting. "Where's the goddamn pass? Where's your pass?" He was a tall man in a wet raincoat and flat cap, and he had a heavy, pink face, the colour of smoked beef. He shouted furiously, "Let go of your bloody balls and get your pass, you bugger."

The man put the lamp down on a table and said, in vernacular, to the other two policemen, "Let me dress, friends."

"What does he say?" Van Den Woud asked them.

"He wants to put on his clothes, *baas*," one of the policemen said.

"Tell him to stop wasting my bloody time. Where's his pass?"

"Your pass, man," the policemen told the naked man. "Your permit to love in this area."

"I will get it," the man replied, sullenly. He turned towards the bed and searched for his trousers. In the bed the woman began to cry in a whimpering noise. The naked man took his time finding his trousers and when he did find them, pulled them on slowly. The woman was crying, and he said something to her, but she did not stop crying.

The man pulled on a tattered shirt and then, stuffing its tails into his trousers, he turned to the police and said, sullenly: "I have no pass."

"What does he say?" Van Den Woud asked, angrily.

"He says that he has no book," the policeman who had not said anything yet, now said.

Constable Van Den Woud looked shocked. "The blerry bastard. Letting us stand here all effing night, and now he says he's got no pass." He stared maliciously at the black man. "God, you'll see, you bogger. You'll see." He turned to one of his men. "Put the handcuffs on him and take him out. I want to search this room. Maybe they've got dagga or kaffir beer here."

The policeman drew his manacles and ordered the man to hold out his wrists, locked them together. He thrust the man towards the door, and the man looked at him and shook his head, saying, "Why do you do this, brother? Why do you do this to your own people?"

Van Den Woud turned to the other policeman and said, "Look around, *jong*. Search the place." He himself went around sweeping things from the top of a packing-case used as a dresser. He came to the bed and with the unemotional movement of a carpenter wrenching a nail, jerked the blanket from the woman's naked body. She began to weep with a high, wailing sound.

Chapter Twenty-Two

The Italians had a battery of mortars set up on the slope across the valley, and were bombarding the road. The valley was yellow and dark-brown and high, a mountain valley, and the road had been cut out of one side of it, opposite the slope where the Italians were. Charlie Pauls lay under the truck with Freda and listened to the thump, thump, thump as the mortar shells exploded along the roadside next to the line of army vehicles. The valley was dark-brown and yellow and the dust rose in thick bursts, and the mortars went thump, thump, thump, and he could feel the pressure of Freda's body through the noise and could hear her saying urgently, but far off:

"Charlie, Charles. People's knocking."

Charlie Pauls woke up slowly, emerging laboriously from sleep which, in spite of dreams, had been soft and soothing as syrup, and came up out into the hot tangle of legs in the bed. The sound of the mortars was still there, but it was not actually that of gun-fire, but was instead the sound of fists beating against the door. He could feel the shack vibrating under the blows, and his eyes opened slowly and with difficulty, like broken blinds.

Somebody outside was yelling, "Open up, *jong,* or we'll break the . . . door down."

And Charlie sat up, disentangling himself from the woman, and shouted: "Awright, awright. I'm coming."

Beside him, Freda was whispering, frightenedly: "What is it, Charlie?"

"Law," he growled. "Got a blerry raid again." Then added, "Is awright. We haven't done nothing." The shack trembled again under the blows, and he shouted once more: "Awright, coming, coming." In the front, outside the curtain that divided the room, the children were wailing with terror.

Charlie groped for his trousers, cursing under his breath. Freda had sat up and was scrabbling around for matches. A light flared, and he grinned at her in the dancing flame.

"Is okay. You see to the children."

He swung off the bed and stood up, pulling on his shirt and jeans. Freda scrambled off the bed, while he struck another match and went around until he found the lamp. Fists started to beat the door again, and he turned up the wick, while Freda sat down on the settee by the whimpering children, whispering to them until they were quiet.

Charlie went barefooted to the door and unlocked it. It was pushed open in his face and he stepped back as uniformed men crowded in. A flash-light dazzled him for a second and then was switched off.

There were four men in the party: a sergeant and three African policemen. The sergeant looked at Charlie Pauls and said, "Alright, *jong, waar's die dagga?* Where's the dope?"

Charlie looked at him and said: "There is no *dagga*, here. We're respectable people."

The sergeant grinned and looked around. He was a short, heavy man with thick, whitish eyebrows that writhed and wriggled when he spoke, like fat maggots curling and uncurling above his eyes, and he had a small, thin mouth, like a bloodless stab wound. For the rest, his face was the colour of red stone and as hard, dissected all over by tiny wrinkles not unlike the lines on a map, spreading over the plains of his cheeks and into the valleys around his mouth, up the hard crag of his nose. His eyes were moist and flat as grey lakes. Beyond him stood the three dark policemen, their faces dull and cow-like.

The sergeant looked around and stared at Freda and the scared faces of the children. Freda clutched the neck of her night-dress, holding it together. Then the sergeant made a sound like a grunt, and pushed past Charlie, stepping over to the curtain. He looked behind the curtain and turned back.

He said, grinning at Charlie: "Nice to be in bed now, hey? Look at me, out in the rain." He grinned at Freda, and then said to Charlie: "What's your name, *jong*?"

"Charles Pauls."

The sergeant made another grunting noise and looked at Freda again with his flat, humourless, moist eyes: "And yours?"

Freda gulped and looked anguished and told him her name. He grinned, showing the edges of his teeth, white as newly painted kerbing. He said to Charlie, "So it's like that, hey? Respectable people." His mouth opened and something clacked and sucked and rattled in the back of his twitching throat. He was laughing. Then he shut his mouth and the sound stopped as if some mechanism had broken down suddenly. He sneered at the woman. "Blerry black whore."

He jerked his wet-capped head at the three motionless constables and headed out through the doorway, into the rainy darkness. The three men followed without a word. Charlie slammed the door after them.

"Law bastards," he snarled, angrily.

Freda was drawing the blankets over the children, her face away from him. He could see her shoulders begin to twitch under the night-dress, and he moved over to her, put a big, splayed hand on a shoulder and turned her towards him. Two tears were sliding from her sleep-puffed eyes down the rounded hillocks of her cheekbones.

He said, frowning, "Hell, what you crying for? They didn't do nothing, did they?"

But she looked at him through the diamond-drops of tears, and her body shook as she said, harshly, "You heard what that one said, didn't you. He said I was a whore." Then she spun from his grasp and ran, shaking, behind the curtain. Charlie stared after her, puzzled, and heard her small, gulping sobbing. He went behind the curtain and she was huddled on the bed, her face to the wall.

Outside the wall the rain was tapping steadily.

He sat on the edge of the sagging bed and scowled at the back quivering under the night-dress. And now love struck him like a blow, slamming into his chest and choking his throat, and he put out the rough hand again, dragging her over onto her back.

He cleared his throat and said awkwardly, "Listen to me, we going to get married. Me and you. Us two." He coughed and looked a little pained and embarrassed. "Don't cry like that now, man, *bokkie*. You'll see. We going to get married. What the hell?"

She gulped and said, "You only saying so."

"No," he said. "True as God. Jesus, we should have been married long ago awready."

Freda whispered, gulping away tears, looking at him: "You mean that, Charlie-boy?"

"Naturally. What do you think?"

"Really, Charlie?"

"Yes, man, woman."

Now, for some reason, he felt himself clear and un-marked, like the pages of a new school-book and it brought him a feeling of embarrassment again. He tried to turn his mind away from it, to think that it was raining outside, and that it was warm and dry here in the little shanty with the papered walls and the lingering heat of the primus stove. The stove needed fixing prop-erly, and he'd see to it. But his mind returned to Freda, like a lost child finding itself home again.

Up the street people were talking noisily in the rain, doors were being pounded and kicked, voices shouted, all the sounds of another world somewhere beyond them. Then he got up suddenly and reached for his old army boots and started to pull them on.

"Charlie," Freda cried. "Where you going?"

"Going to see what goes on."

"You mustn't. There might be trouble."

He said, stamping to get the boots on, "Don't go on like that. I'm just going to see. To see what's happening to our people."

"Charlie, man."

"I won't get into trouble," he told her. "You just lie still and see the children don't cry." He wrestled into the oilskin slicker and smiled at her and winked.

"You'll see."

Outside was a glare of headlamps of several riot vans which had penetrated the settlement and had parked in the small cramped, muddy square. Dogs were bark-ing furiously, and there were figures moving about in the steady downpour. The police had collected a number of prisoners, and they stood huddled together, dripping and shivering, while they were sorted out and then ordered into the backs of the trucks.

An African man came out of his cabin to the gate of his yard in order to see what was going on. He was wearing an old overcoat over his pyjamas. Light fell on him, and he was surrounded by police.

"Where's your reference book, kaffir?"

"It is inside, in my coat pocket."

"Where is it, man? You should have it on you."

"I will get it. It is inside."

"No pass, hey? Come, come on, come on."

"Listen, it is inside, sir."

But hands were laid on him and he was led towards where others stood waiting to be loaded into the police trucks.

There was a crowd of African and Coloured men and a few women, waiting in the rain to be loaded and driven away. Many had been taken for not having documents, or whose documents were not in order – the absence of a rubber stamp could change a life. Others had been found in possession of *dagga,* some had resisted the police search. There were also those who had been found to be selling liquor illicitly.

Charlie saw Aunty Mina with the group of prisoners. She was remonstrating with an officer, shouting at him and waving a dripping umbrella so that he shied away from her, laughing. Thick and dark as an oak, Aunty Mina stormed at the officer.

"Look here, captain, I'm not giving a damn what you say about it, but what for I'm standing in this rain? You tell me."

The officer laughed. He was arrogantly cheerful, and thought this fat old aunty was rather fun. He had had altercations with her before. He laughed, "Alright,

Mina. We'll give you a nice dry van all to yourself. Then you can have a private cell until you appear before the magistrate."

Aunt Mina poked the umbrella at him. It had broken in the wind and rain and now consisted of a handle, a flap of cloth, and several frightful spikes, dangerous as some medieval instrument of torture. The officer reared backwards, fearful of his eyes.

"I'm not frighting for your magistrate, colonel. I paid seven fines awready and I can pay seven more. There! What I'm wanting to know, is what for in this rain, hey? You tell me." She possessed the ferocity of an old African buffalo.

Some of the prisoners laughed, nervously. The officer shook his head, laughing, and said, "Alright, Mina. Alright."

It was raining steadily, but not hard, and Charlie Pauls stood in the half-light on the edge of the glare of the headlamps and watched the scene. The rain rapped against his yellow slicker and ran off it in trickles, dripped from the peak of his cap. Police were counting off prisoners into the trucks, shouting at them, waving flash-lights and truncheons.

Somebody said, sharply: "What you standing around here for, *jong*?"

Charlie looked aside and there was a policeman watching him. Under the shiny bill of his flat uniform cap his eyes had the look of dead cinders in the shadows, and he had a blonde moustache, pearly with raindrops. He wore pistol harness over his wet raincoat.

"You got any business here, man?"

"Just looking," Charlie said, and feeling suddenly malicious, grinned at the policeman through the wet stubble on his face.

"Move off," the policeman said. "Go home. Eff off."

Something smouldered inside Charlie and now he said, stiffly: "I'm just looking. Can't a man watch his own people being effed off to jail?"

"Oh," the constable said, his moustache moving as he spoke. "Oh, a hardcase bastard, *ne*?" His hands started to grope for the handcuffs on his belt while his shadowy eyes watched Charlie.

Charlie said, his voice surly: "Okay, I'm hardcase. Now what then?"

"Bet you're one of those Communist troublemakers. I'll show you."

Charlie grinned insolently through his surliness. His eyes watched the constable's hands. They were big and red, the colour of wet ham, as they fumbled with the handcuffs. Then the policeman turned his face slightly, to call for assistance, and Charlie hit him suddenly on the exposed jawbone.

It was a hard, snapping blow, with all his weight behind it, and the policeman's feet left the ground and his back struck it with a hard, muddy, plopping sound, as if he had been dropped from a great height. Then Charlie was off, past the flaying khaki-clad legs, heading for the darkness.

Behind him he heard the policeman yell, and then a chorus of yells. Feet stumbled through the mud as more police came up, shouting. But Charlie was a yellow blur through the darkness, dodging and ducking like a whippet.

One of the police raised his service pistol and fired. The shot made a flat, snapping sound in the rain and the flare of the muzzle gashed the dripping light of the headlamps, while the echo of the gunshot ka-yapped among the shanties.

Charlie was gone, into the jungle of shacks. He skidded down an alleyway, climbed over a low tin fence, and sat down against it. He knew that if he kept on running he might come up against other police searching the settlement. So he sat in the mud in the rain and recovered his breath. He thought. That was a nice blow, never ever got one in like that. Then he began to laugh. He laughed silently, his body shaking under the yellow oilskin.

Since he was no longer near the congregation of prisoners, he could not see police bring his brother, Ronald, into the light of the trucks.

Chapter Twenty-Three

Ronald was just about to step down the muddy, leaf-strewn embankment on the edge of the road, on his frustrated wandering about the dark settlement, when he saw the girl, Susie Meyer, emerge from under the watery light of the canopy of George Mostert's garage. For a moment he was startled, and stopped short under the growth of trees that dripped down on him, staring at the girl crossing the road. Then anger, unreasonable, tore at him with sharp claws, and he stumbled along the roadway, to head her off. The rain was beginning to fall faster now, a regular, straight downpour, but Ronald did not feel the soaking chill, for his guts were hot with rage.

The girl slithered off the road, hunched in her tawdry bright clothes under a second-hand overcoat with an exhausted collar, and the soaked head-scarf. She was almost on the old street when Ronald burst out of the brush in front of her.

She gave a little hiccuping cry of fright, jerking upright. Then she recognised the face thrust near hers in the gloom, raindrops sliding over its enraged anonymity, and she cried: "Oh, it's you. Oo, you gave me a scare."

A hand closed over her arm and pulled her towards a dripping tree. "I gave you a scare, *ne*? I *reckon* I gave you a scare, Susie."

"Hey, let me go, *jong*. What you think you doing, man?"

"I'll let you go awright. When I'm finish." He peered past her, towards the horizon of pale light above the banked side of the road, where George Mostert's service station stood under the running sky. "So you's *mos* going in for *that* stuff, hey? Reckon I caught you cold-blood."

"What stuff? I got to go. Is raining, man."

". . . the rain. You know what stuff. That burg's *mos* got a car and a business and cash, you reckon, hey?"

Now Susie Meyer understood and glanced in the direction of the road. Malice brought a comforting sensation, and she smiled at him in the gloom. She was at home with malice, it was a part of her, like lipstick and curling-pins.

She said: "Well, what about it? You my boss? I can do *mos* what I like, don't I say?"

"You reckon?" His voice was harsh, the sound of cinders trodden underfoot. His hand tightened on her arm, but she was smiling tauntingly at him, her eyes bright and mocking as artificial jewels.

"Oh, yes, I do reckon. It was nice. We had drinks, and he got records, too. Bings and others."

"Blerry white crack." His face contorted between tears and rage, humiliation squeezed him in a shameful grip. "You was supposed to *jol* with me. You my girl, isn't it?"

"*Garn.* I can do as I please. Who you reckon you are, bossing me about? Now let me go, I don't bother with lighties no more." And she burst into laughter, a hideous, ecstatic sound that caught at his nerves like a blunt saw, and his free hand clenched on the half-crown jack-knife he carried in his coat pocket.

She laughed and laughed, twisting to free herself, but his hand jerked her forward, gripping hard before she could recoil, and while she was still laughing the knife slashed out, as he yelped like a hurt dog.

The rain beat down on her and she felt the burn of the knifeblade in her breast, through the chill of the rain. The blade slashed and thrust, slicing her face and driving into her chest again. She tried to scream, but it was a retching sound for the knife had already cut into her throat, through flesh and wind-pipe and vocal cords. The force of the stabbing knocked her, floundering, into the mud. She fell heavily on her side and tried to scramble away, but she was helplessly pinned down. The blade was stabbing into her body again and again, through the cheap, bright clothes and into the taut flesh, bursting into it. Her arms would not lift and she could not stop the knife. Under the savage, enraged, cutting caresses of the blade she could do nothing but surrender as to another lover.

Ronald gaped down at the huddle of old clothes at his feet. He could not see it clearly in the dark. There was something bounding up and down inside him, like some monstrous spring gone wild. He tried to say something, but it came out as the same sounds the dying girl had made. He was still standing over her, goggling, when the police flash-lights washed over him and over the girl, so that the dead eyes stared up out of the split, rain-washed face like lustreless pearls.

Chapter Twenty-Four

Lying on the mattress in the corner of the packing-case shack, Caroline heard the rain splashing outside, and felt the pain come upon her again. The pains had been coming during the afternoon and all evening, but she had kept it to herself, trying to push it out of her mind, feeling more shy than scared. She should have been frightened by the pains, this being her first pregnancy, but her mind was as stolid and bovine as her face and body. But now the contractions lashed at her with the bite of barbed-wire; she bit her lower lip, her great body twitching beneath the old blanket and the overcoat.

The shack was small and cluttered. She and Alfy slept on the old mattress on the floor, and there was an old washstand that filled one end of the room, with a chipped and leprous enamel basin and jug on it, and a candle on a wooden box they used as a table; and their clothes hung from a wire line strung along the low ceiling. There was a pile of old newspapers Ma had told her to gather for the confinement, and above it a picture of the Crucifixion in a cracked frame, with Christ lolling easily on the cross, as if asleep, watched by two Roman soldiers in red cloaks and leaning on spears. There was also a picture pasted up on the boards of a film star in a cowboy outfit which Alfy had cut from a magazine. The handsome face, covered with a sort of outbreak of measles caused by fly-spots, smiled into the camp cabin.

An old-fashioned oil-lamp hung from the ceiling and Alfy crouched under it on a rickety apple-box, reading a tattered paperback in its oily light. The shack smelled of mouldy clothes, smoke and dampness, and the icy air whistled through open joints.

Pain jabbed Caroline again, and she clutched at her swollen stomach as a moan burst from her lips. Alfred, engrossed in gun-fights and rustlers, heard the sound through the drive of the rain and the imaginary bark of six-shooters. He looked up, startled.

"Hey, Ca'line, what's the matter, hey? What do you need, hey?" He sprang to his feet; fatherhood loomed up over him like a frightening Frankenstein, and he scrambled towards his wife, his eyes wide.

"Ma," Caroline gasped, between spasms. "Fetch Ma."

He was already wrestling his coat feverishly from the line across the room. Some clothes fell off, onto the floor, and he kicked them out of the way, struggling into the coat. "Is it bad, Ca'line? You just lie still, hear? You lie still. I'll call Ma."

He pulled open the door. The wood had swelled and he tugged in a panic. A gust of rain swept in as he finally got it open, and the candle on the wooden box went out. Alfred plunged out and wrestled the door shut after him. Caroline lay under the blanket on the floor, in the meagre light of the oil lamp, and held herself, shivering, waiting for the next snap of pain.

Caroline groaned as pain tore like knives into her loins, and a fine sweat sprang out on her forehead, sprayed there by the atomiser of childbirth. She started to weep and sobs shook her, while she wished Ma would come. She was afraid that she was going to die, and she wailed with the fear and the sharp spasms. The rain drummed down and a leak started in the plank ceiling where some of the tar-paper had split along a seam. The water dripped in and formed a puddle in front of the doorway, and spread across the floor.

When Ma came at last, she had an old coat over her shoulders and was carrying the storm lamp from Charlie's room. She shut the door and looked about, then smiled gently at the girl on the mattress.

"Now, now, is awright, child."

Ma took off her wet coat and dropped it against the wall by the door, then she looked around again until she found some projection and hung the lamp from it, turning up the flame. Then she turned up the other lamp, too, and went to the wash-stand. She lifted the jug and brought it under the leak in the ceiling, placing it on the floor so that the rain-water raised a small clamour as it ran in.

Ma knelt down by Caroline and wiped her forehead with a cloth.

"How long you been having pains, child?" Caroline moaned and babbled and Ma said, "There. You should have told me early. We could have took you to the house. Now, you see? You got to have it right here." She clucked and smiled with the old, dry lips.

The pains were coming close, and Caroline abandoned herself completely now that Ma was there, and screamed.

"Awright, awright," Ma said. "I sent Alfy for the nurse, and to tell Nzuba to come over. She always he'p with these things." The rain roared against the shack. "I hope the nurse come in time."

She turned to the pile of newspapers and started to unpack it. "Don't you push, hey. Don't push yet."

It was warmer in the room now, with the two turned-up lamps. Smoke drifted against the ceiling, and the leak rattled into the jug on the floor. Caroline cried out again and again.

Ma pulled the blanket and coat up over the girl's body and rolled the old dress she slept in, up to her waist. "Now you got to lift yourself, hey, so I can get the papers under you. I wish Nzuba would come. Now, can you do it?"

Caroline screamed again, and moaned. The sounds hung for a moment in the shack. The pounding of the rain dropped suddenly, and came in intermittent gusts, swishing along the walls and the roof, and the leak in the ceiling subsided to a tinkle, like a tap being turned down.

Then the door creaked and whined and Missus Nzuba edged her way into the shack. Her mountainous bulk almost filled the entire space, and she clucked with a sound that seemed to come from some gigantic bird.

"Ai, ai, 's awright, 's awright," she cried. Her vast-ness made the floor sag, but she was lightfooted as a dancer. "How, this rain."

"I's glad you come, Nzuba," Ma said. "I put on hot water, and there's old papers here."

"Ai, little gal," the woman said, kneeling by the mattress. She looked as if she would plunge right through the wall if by accident she overbalanced. But, ponderous as a hippopotamus, she possessed the skill of a conjuror, working expertly over Caroline, and saying, "Oh, oh, oh," sympathetically, as the girl cried out.

"Will she be awright?" Ma asked, anxiously.

"How, she is strong as a young cow," Missus Nzuba said. "Not to worry, Pauls. Not to worry. We wait, that is all."

"She left it late," Ma said. "I hope Alfy hurry up."

On the mattress Caroline heaved with a shudder that

gripped her loins, and her thighs drew back and then straightened and drew back again, tightly, and she cried out, gripping wildly at the women, and she cried out as the water broke and drenched the padding of papers under her.

Through the crying, the pounding of a hand against the door came like the sound of drum-beats. A voice was shouting, "*Maak oop,* open up. Open up inside there."

"Who can that be?" Ma asked. "Not the nurse, yet. But I hope so."

The hand pounded the door again, and it shook as if with a palsy. Ma got up and went over and drew the bolt. A flash-light burst into her face and she saw the ponchoed figures in the dark beyond the pale white face of the policeman.

"Awright," he said. "What's all this shouting in here? You all drunk? Where's the wine?" He started to advance, but Ma blocked his way, standing firmly, looking up at the lardwhite face and the eyes as grey as ash under the uniform cap.

"You can't come in," she said, sternly. "My daughter is having a baby."

"Baby? Whatter baby?"

"There's a girl having a baby here," Ma told him again.

At that moment Caroline screamed. The police raider said, "*Ghod!*" He peered past Ma into the shack, saw Missus Nzuba's vastness crouched over the girl on the mattress. His eyes moved about, over the smoky ceiling, the muddy floor, the leak in the roof and the ragged clothes displayed as if for sale. The smell of smoke and oil and birth made the air fetid.

He said, again: "Baby? What, in here?" Then he

shrugged and growled, "Awright, awright." He turned and snapped orders at his men, while Ma shut the door on him.

Later Caroline cried out again, her legs straining, and Missus Nzuba said to Ma, "Head is showing awready."

Ma said, anxiously, "You reckon is awright? The nurse –"

"Is awright," the massive woman said. "We know about these things. We know it, Pauls."

The girl screamed and strained, and the two women worked over her. Out in the dark, the police convoy was moving away, tyres hissing like vipers in the mud, lurching drunkenly over ruts and stones. They had turned the settlement inside out, as one would a coat, shaken out the pockets, examined its lining, like a miser searching for a lost coin, and now they muttered and roared away under the slanting rain.

Chapter Twenty-Five

The rubbish dump along the edge of the settlement is a favourite playground of the children. They can climb dunes of soggy paper and rags, and clamber over the jungle-gyms of rusting iron, see-saw on lengths of decaying and slippery flotsam, breathing the air of disease dotted with flies like currants in a pudding.

From the mouldering corpse of the dump project gaunt, crumbling ribs of discarded machinery, broken furniture, and tangled entrails of rusty wire. Here lay fantastic fragments of ruined and abandoned material; a house door that led nowhere, and a section of drainage pipe that is a marvellous echo chamber. Maggots squirm and burrow in the dark paste of putrefying wood, and various insects inhabit the curved world of broken shards of porcelain or tin cans. There are rusty railway lines, bent and twisted like plants from another planet, and the buckled body of an ancient car, gaping like the jaws of some strange monster.

All the things on the dump are the utterly useless cast-offs, the final waste matter from the giant bowels of the slum. For every little or large element which is of some mysterious value or utility has been carried off. Somebody throws away a cracked lavatory pan, and somebody else picks it up to use as a flower pot. The dump is a monstrous exchange mart. There is wealth even in dirt. Once a new-born baby, strangled and wrapped in bloody newspapers had been found there.

Actually, a wandering mongrel had been the first to make the discovery, and was in the process of devouring it, when some human had happened along.

The rain has stopped again, and the children play along the dump, hurling aloft confetti of tattered rags and soaked paper, cheering shrilly in ancient child-voices.

"Here's a wake-up pisspot," cries one of them, and puts it on his head like a helmet. "Ten-shun!"

"Gwan, go and blow. You reckon you a *soldat*?"

"Don't I say? I can shoot you dead, *mos*."

"You reckon, hey? My Darra was a soldier, a real one, man. What you know?"

"Awright, awright. Jorny-boy's *boeta* Charlie was also a soldier. Ask him."

Jorny Pauls swells with pride. "You know then. Charlie was a *soldat, mos*. Was in the war, also, a long time ago, already. Don't I say?" Something strikes him and he cries, "Hell, man, my other brother, Ronny-boy, killed a goose. He's in jail now, reckon and think. Chopped her dead with a knife." And he stabs himself in the belly with a grubby finger and screams in a mockery of assassination, staggering about the hill of muck. Everybody laughs, and he cries, proudly: "Further, Charlie reckon they might hang Ronny-boy up on a rope." He clasps his hands about his throat, choking and gurgling, while the others shout and chuckle with glee.

A little boy shouts, "Hey, *rookers*, I found a gun." And he brandishes an old piece of pipe-joint, firing at the others. "*Khhhh. Khhhh.*"

The party around Jorny breaks up, and he scowls disappointedly, then goes to join them to admire the new-found toy.

"We play teckies and burgs. I'm the head tec."

"*Garn*, look at him. Head tec. *Garn*."

"Ah, come on, men. Don't come out ape, hey."

"Awright then. I'll be head burg then. Come on, come on." They set off through the screen of flies, screaming like frightened seagulls.

A lone carnation grows on the dump. Gestated in the ooze and the slime and watery filth, its green stem rises against the side of a tilting flap of iron. Against the flaking brown rust, its bright, scarlet bugle rears in the pallid sunlight. Its beautiful, wrinkled and intricately folded petals are bright with tiny drops of moisture, clear and bright as diamonds. The flower stands alone, gleaming, wonderfully bright, red as blood and life, like hope blooming in an anguished breast.

Chapter Twenty-Six

The rain had stopped, but the sky was rumpled with dirty grey cloud. In the morning the light was pale and white, without warmth, forcing its way through the great barriers of cumulus, shining dully on the pools and little lakes among the shacks. The people looked from the doorways and waited for the rain to come again.

In Freda's shanty it was warm and dry. She kept the primus stove going most of the time, and the cardboard and paper-covered walls kept the heat in. Now Freda pumped the stove, and it popped and sputtered like a fire-cracker, and the circular flame burst into a yellow-blue stuttering. She propped up the stove with an empty match-box where one of its legs was missing. Satisfied, she buttoned the purple coat presented to her a long time ago by madam, and spoke to the children.

One of the children, a little boy, had cut his foot on a piece of glass at the rubbish dump; he sat dejectedly on the settee, scowling at the blood-stained rag.

"Now, I don't want you to get up to no trouble," she told them. "Gracie, you look after Klonky. His foot is sore, so no one of you can go out. Anyway, I'm going to lock the door so you can't run away from him. I just going to the shop."

"Yes, ma," the little girl said.

"I shall not be long," Freda said. "So you two be good. Maybe I'll buy you each one a penny sugarstick."

"Yes, ma," the little girl said, and smiled shyly.

"Awright. Is cold outside, anyway, and the stove is nice and warm."

Straightening her scarf, she went out and dragged the door shut and locked it. She put the key in her purse with her small change, and went down the muddy lane under the watching and waiting sky. The wind swished through the trees, waving their mustard-yellow flowers like fans, and rattled loose the walls and flapping sheets of tin.

Over in a little square, African women had set up their stalls to display piles of offal for sale; sheep's heads, and heaps of tripe arranged in rows on tables of boards and boxes or old oil drums. Flies hovered over the meat, gorging themselves on dried blood, and the women flapped their hands, dry and brown as bundles of twigs, to drive off the flies, while they chatted or called to likely customers.

Among the shanties, people moved carefully over the puddles and lakes, like explorers traversing some dangerous swampland, edging through the jungle of rusty tin and leaning wood-frames, past cloying orchids that were latrines, and through the thorny undergrowth of wire fences and jaggedly-spined railings. Overhead the sky lurked in ambush, treacherous as a bog.

In the hut, the children imagined that their mother was staying away a very long time. The promise of sugarsticks nagged at them, and they fidgeted impatiently. Klonky, the little boy, thought they should make a tent of the settee cover and pretend to be camping. But the little girl, Gracie, turned down the suggestion, saying that the mother would be cross and wouldn't give them the sugarsticks, not until tomorrow, perhaps.

"I want a piece of bread, then," Klonky whined.

"Hold your mouth," Gracie snapped. "You always wanting to eat, eat, eat."

"I'm going to tell ma you don't want to give me a piece of bread," the boy whimpered.

"Awright, awright," the girl said, pulling a face and sticking her tongue out at him. She crossed to the table where part of a loaf stood by the basin of dishes and the primus stove. The stove roared and growled and popped like a faulty engine. The little girl picked up a knife and started to saw at the bread. The table shook on the uneven dung floor. The shaking upset the match-box prop, and the stove toppled over with a clang. Then it exploded.

The old, clogged, faulty stove, dangerous as a mine, went off with a slapping bang, like the bursting of an immense paperbag, exploding like shrapnel and sending pieces of hot brass and iron hurtling in all directions. Burning oil spat into the little girl's face, set alight her clothes and danced up into her hair. Flames ran like water across the table and caught at the dry paper and cardboard lining of the wall. The wall crackled into life. The child shrieked in an atrocious agony and rushed blindly into the curtain across the room. The curtain caught alight from the blazing torch of her body, and screaming, the child tore it down, and doing so, dragged it into the oil lamp hanging from a nail in the ceiling. Oil splashed everywhere; it caught the screaming boy who was trying to hobble on one foot to the door, and washed him in a bath of dancing yellow as he plucked frantically at the lock.

The children shrieked and danced an awful jig until fumes and fire choked them, boiled their skin into blisters, spluttered through layers of fat, roasted flesh,

157

cartilage and membranes; roared and snapped and snarled at the lining of the room, the scanty furniture, the cocoanut-hair settee, mattresses, blankets, the bed, everything. The shack, its insides burnt away, the wooden supports ablaze, sagged and lurched like a drunkard.

Flame and heat, first red, then yellow, then searing white devoured the interior swiftly, and the tin walls flopped and groaned as if in agony, hot sheets smoking, and woodwork sending up pyrotechnics of sparks.

Outside there was an uproar. Men and women rushed, shouting and screaming, towards the blaze, slipping and splashing through puddles. They heard the shrieks of the children, but the appalling sounds died quickly. Now the heat and the fire snarled at them, holding them at bay. Two men edged forward, but the flames thrust them back. No one dared approach the pyre. Men and women ran about in horrified circles, clutched at each other and at their hair, aghast. Then the remnants of the shack collapsed with a flapping sound as of a thousand cranes taking off in flight, and hissed like an engine where parts of it touched the wet mud. Overhead the sky sneered.

And through the cries and the crackle of embers came another sound. At first it was a wail, and then it became a sort of shrill, horrid gobbling chant, an awful sound-picture which might conjure up the abominable death-rites of some primitive tribe. It rose to a high, nerve-plucking ululation which was something more than a scream or a shriek, the sound of an impossible sadness, a sound beyond agony, an outcry of unendurable woe, forlorn beyond comprehension, a sort of grief beyond grief. It was Freda.

Struggling in the grip of several men and women, her

bolting eyes stared at the smoking ruins, while she tried to tear out tufts of her hair and the sound came from her wide-open mouth.

Charlie was crying, "Freda, Freda, Freda. No. No. No," clutching at one of her arms while everybody set up an incoherent clamour.

Then, Charlie, suddenly recalling the hysteria of men under bombardment, released her arm, and stepping back, struck her swiftly on the side of the jaw.

Freda hung limply in supporting hands, and Charlie said, gently, "I'll take her up to our place. I reckon that's the only place for her now."

Chapter Twenty-Seven

On the curve of the main road to the north, George Mostert's Service Station and Garage stood like a beggar waiting for somebody to toss a coin into his cup. Lonely as a lazar-house, its grime-covered walls bore a look of scabrous abandonment. And from the glass-fronted office, George Mostert himself stared out past the cloud-banks of finger-marks, and watched for the intermittent traffic. His mind, bored and empty, registered each vehicle, idly filing away each brand and make, like papers into their respective pigeon-holes: that's a Diamond T; there goes a Ford, old car, 1939 model; that one's a Dodge.

A massive transport truck roared past, its horn blaring on the curve, thrusting aside oncoming traffic with hurried irritability. Sometime later, a small sports car slammed past, and Mostert had a glimpse of red hair whipped in the wind and mouth agape with fear and laughter beside the grinning driver.

Then, to his surprise, he saw the long, low, smart new station-wagon slow down and slide up to the petrol pumps. As he scrambled to his feet, his mind automatically registered the make of the car. Then he was outside, shambling across the slippery apron, a light of pleasure turned up like a wick inside him.

A man climbed out of the station-wagon and came towards him. A woman sat in front, staring idly ahead. The handsome, pudgy, artificially-preserved face was aglow with health and complacency, pink-white and smooth, the colour of blood-and-cream. The red mouth seemed to pant a little.

"Afternoon," George Mostert said to the driver.

"Hullo," the man replied. He was short and plump, and his healthy layers of fat lay comfortably all over him, so that the original lines of his body were lost in the soft curves. He wore a smart overcoat and he had whitish hair, thinning, and a shiny, pink face. "Ah, fill her up," he said, and smiled at George Mostert. "The special, please." He had an air of condescension about him, as if he realised that he was doing the business a great favour. He glanced around at the peeling shabbiness, the stack of worn tyres, the tattered advertisements and a broken novelty-propeller spinning slowly above the dusty bottles of lubrication oil.

"Business not so good, eh?" he observed, handing George Mostert the key of the tank. His hand was plump and smooth, pinkish and covered with fine fuzz, like a peach.

George Mostert lifted down the hose. He was a little annoyed at the man's observation, and it dampened what little pleasure his company might have inspired.

"Nope," he mumbled, under his breath, unlocking the shiny top of the tank. There was a pile of luggage in the back of the station-wagon. George Mostert thrust the nozzle into the tank and watched the indicator on the pump.

"Lucky I ran into you," the man said. "Left town in a hurry and forgot to fill up. Wife got a bloody telegram her old woman died, so she had to decide to attend the bloody funeral." He spoke quietly, so that the woman could not overhear. He winked generously at George Mostert. "Mother-in-bloody-law."

George Mostert grinned momentarily under his ragged moustache, quick grimace, like a slide hurriedly shown on a screen. He said with a kind of pride, "That's one complaint I haven't got."

"Ha, ha," the man chuckled. "You all alone around here?" He glanced around again, casually.

"Yes."

"Oh. Look, you might as well check the tyres, too."

"Right-o, sir."

He wandered around the sleek, shining metal of the station-wagon and gazed across the road. Beyond the opposite edge and the growth of brushwood, the roofs of the shantytown were scattered like grey and brown rocks along a coastline. A cloud of smoke was dwindling in the white-grey air above it.

"What's that?" he asked of George Mostert.

The woman turned her head and said, impatiently: "Harold, how *long* are we going to stay here? We *must* be getting on."

"In a moment, dear," the plump man said, and smiled at her.

"That?" George Mostert said, coming around with the pressure gauge in his hand. "Oh, jus' one of those slum places."

"Christ, I bet it's mucky as hell. Wonder why the authorities don't clear the bloody lot out. Just brings disease and things." He stared out across the road. "If I had any say, I'd pull down the whole bally lot and clear 'em all out." He shook his head and the wisps of hair, like straw, fluttered. "I don't know what we poor buggers pay taxes for."

"Tyres 're okay, I reckon," George Mostert said. "Rain treats those people pretty bad."

The man looked at the indicator on the pump and

fetched out a wallet, thick with notes, counting off the amount. "I can just imagine how those poor buggers live." He spoke as if he was a connoisseur of poverty. "Well, there you are." He placed the bills in George Mostert's grease-lined, broken-nailed hand, and added some silver to make up the exact sum. Then, as an afterthought, he added a half-crown. "Well, that's that."

"Thanks a million, sir," George Mostert said.

The man waved a hand at him and went around to the driving side. Under his smart, tailored overcoat his plump behind rolled like a woman's. The motor coughed into life and dropped to a throaty purr, like a well-fed tiger. George Mostert watched the station-wagon swing away.

As they reached out along the concrete road, the woman said, "What a slowcoach that man was."

"Oh, he didn't take too long," her husband said. "Sort of surly devil, though."

"And such a dirty place. You should have filled up in town. I told you."

"Well, I forgot. Anyway, petrol is petrol, isn't it?"

Overhead the sky broke and it began to rain. This time it was a hard, efficient rain, driving down and splashing high on the concrete of the road, drumming on the top of the station-wagon. It sheeted down, hiding the landscape. The plump man switched on the wind-screen wipers and they drove steadily north in the comforting warmth of the car's interior.

George Mostert watched the station-wagon out of sight, and then turned back towards his office, moving with his shambling gait. Behind him the rain bounced on the roadway. Before him the door of the little glass office waited, as inevitable as the grave.

Inside, he turned on the light, for the rain had brought a gloom with it, and rang the cash register. He tossed the money inside and pushed the drawer shut. Then he opened a drawer of his desk and got out a brandy bottle. He poured himself a stiff tot into a cracked tumbler. When he swallowed the liquor, it was without enjoyment. He drank without pleasure, as if he needed the alcohol only to anaesthetize the bitterness and solitude that gnawed at him, persistent as a toothache.

He peered out towards the world, like an entombed miner through a gap in a rockfall, surrounded by the dusty piles of advertising literature, the spike of dog-eared accounts, and the smudged calendar covered with long-forgotten phone numbers.

Chapter Twenty-Eight

In the north-west the rainheads piled up, massing in bulging grey towers that moved across the sky, and even the pale light faded, crushed by the ponderous mass, leaving only a hard, metallic gloom through the driving rain. The fat drops of rain hurtled down and the wind slanted them, turning the rain into grey, diagonal corrugations, and there was a biting chill in the wind.

The afternoon was a silver-grey alloy of rain and clouds, and the clouds came lower until the sky was evil with them, and the greyness stretched from horizon to horizon. The rain chattered and growled and the clouds broke again and again, tumbling the water earthwards in a gigantic cataract.

At first the rain swept and puttered on the roofs of the shacks and the cabins, then, thrust on by the clouds behind, and slanted by the wind, it roared and drummed, leaning against the sheeted sides of the houses and slashing at the seams of the roofs. In the lanes and the hollow squares, the water rose under the grey rosettes of raindrops. The rain filled the ruts and the channels, and the lanes and squares overflowed, and the water crept across the dooryards and against the scanty foundations of huts and lean-tos, and all the time the sky cracked and split and crashed.

The rain tore at a roof and the wind lifted it and took it, spinning and gambolling, through mid air, a monstrous scythe that sheared through tree-tops and scrub and tore away flimsy fences. The rain scrabbled at the side of a house, groping at a weak overlap, a loosened seam, found a hold and clung on, tugging and jerking, until rusty nails and bailing-wire surrendered and the rain and the wind ripped away a great flap of tin and wood, and left the interior of the shanty exposed like the side of a shrapnel-sheared face, showing all the bloody convolutions of brain, ear and muscle which were drenched furniture, huddled people and slapping pieces of sacks.

The rain excavated foundations and dredged through topsoil and a house sagged and tottered, battered into a jagged rhomboid of gaping seams and banging sides. The rain gurgled and bubbled and chuckled in the eaves and ran like quicksilver along the ceilings, and below, the shivering poor blew on their braziers and stoked their fires, crouched trembling with ague in the relentless dampness, huddled together for warmth and clenching their teeth against the pneumonic chattering.

In the Pauls house, those inside heard the rain, but took no notice of it. It was a sound apart from the feeling of sorrow. Miraculously, the house held. Dad and Charlie Pauls and others had built it well; well enough to stand up against this kind of storm, anyway. The rain lashed at it, as if in an anger of frustration. Finding the leak in the ceiling blocked, the water steered towards the ends of the roof and seeped down the walls inside. But the house seemed to clench its teeth and cling defiantly to life.

The old iron stove which Charlie and Dad had dragged four miles down the road, boomed and roared and the fire inside it spread its warmth. The house groaned and winced in agony under the whip of the rain, and the floor sagged, but held on.

Ma Pauls sat in her chair in the bedroom and rocked

slowly backwards and forward, her body hunched and her face withered with sadness. She sang in her old mind, and thought back on Dad Pauls, on young Ronald, on Freda's children. Her hands, corded and dry, like skeins of brown wool, were clasped in her lap, as she rocked.

On the bed where Dad Pauls had died, Freda lay now, her face ugly with sorrow and shock. Ma had made her comfortable as could be, and had given her sugar and water to drink in order to drive off the shock. She had sent the bewildered, horror-stricken people away, and had sent Alfred to sit with Caroline and the baby.

Charlie stood at the window and stared blindly out at the grey world. He wanted to say something. He wanted to say something kind and beautiful to Freda, but words failed him and he felt empty now, empty and limp as a discarded coat.

Charlie was tall and had the big shoulders and chest of a man who had worked for years with a pick and shovel, and the muscles of his body bunched and knotted under the old khaki shirt. His thick, solid jaw ran into a curved chin, brown and hard as mahogany, and his hollow cheeks were blurred with stubble. But for all his strength, he felt weak and abandoned.

Freda stirred on the bed and moaned, and said in a whispering sob, "I locked the door. I locked the door. Maybe –"

"Freda, Freda," Charlie whispered.

"I locked the door," she moaned.

"Yes," he told her, gently. "Awright, you locked the door. But I could have fixed the stove. You asked me to, and I didn't do it. So don't blame yourself, *bokkie*." Words came from him now, suddenly, as if a blocked pipe had been cleared. He said: "Hell, man, maybe we is both to blame. Maybe it was all just put out like that, the way some people say. Maybe is God. Uncle Ben and *ou* Brother Bombata talk like that. I don't know, for sure, Freda." He cleared his throat and took her hand. It wasn't cold, as he had expected it to be, but rough and warm with life.

"Listen," he said. "There was this *rooker* I worked with when we was laying pipe up country. A *slim* burg, I reckon. A clever fellow. Always was saying funny things. He said something one time, about people most of the time takes trouble hardest when they alone. I don't know how it fit in here, hey. I don't understand it real right, you see. But this burg had a lot of good things in his head, I reckon." He paused, and then stumbled on, his voice a little sad. "Like he say, people can't stand up to the world alone, they got to be together. I reckon maybe he was right. A *slim juba*. Maybe it was like that with Ronny-boy. Ronald didn't ever want nobody to he'p him. Wanted to do things alone. Never was a part of us. I don't know. Maybe, like Uncle Ben, too. Is not natural for people to be alone. Hell, I reckon people was just *made* to be together. I –" Words failed him again, and he shook his head, frowning.

He looked down at Freda, and saw that she had been crying silently. Tears made tiny, sparkling pools reflecting the lamplight in the hollows of her eyes and the corners of her mouth. He was aware that her hand held his tightly, and he put the other hand over it and patted the warm brown skin of the back of hers.

Charlie said, feeling awkward, the awkwardness of the time he had decided to marry her: "Look, you just lie still, hey. I'll go and make some cawfee for us. Reckon we can spare some cawfee on a' afternoon like this." He smiled at her and released his hand.

168

Ma was quiet, her hands clasped and she looked as if she was praying.

Charlie went out of the room and the floor groaned under his weight. In his bedroom, the boy, Jorny, was curled up in Ronald's bed. Water was soaking down the walls in the house. Charlie thought he'd have to go on the roof again, as soon as this rain stopped.

It was warmer in the kitchen, and when he uncovered the stove the flames leaped up at him. He moved about, his head bent under the lowness of the ceiling. He spooned coffee into the kettle from the tin, and poured water from the bucket onto it. Then he set the kettle over the flames, and waited for the coffee to boil.

Feeling in the pocket of his jeans, he found his cigarette tin and drew one. He straightened the cigarette between his thick, calloused fingers, and then with a twist of paper burning from the stove, he lighted the cigarette. He leaned against the kitchen table and smoked, waiting for the kettle to boil.

After a while he was listening to the rain pounding against the roof and the sides of the house. Then he moved to the kitchen door and, drawing the bolt, opened it a little way. A gust drove the rain into his face.

Charlie Pauls stood there and looked out into the driving rain. The rain bored into the earth. The light outside was grey, and the rain fell steadily, like heartbeats. As he looked out at the rain, he saw to his surprise, a bird dart suddenly from among the patchwork roofs of the shanties and head straight, straight into the sky.

GLOSSARY

baas	boss, master
bedonerd	crazy, mixed up
blerry	bloody
blik	tin
bliksem	miscreant, devil
boet	brother
boeta	big brother
bok	girl friend
bokkie	more intimate expression for girl friend
brandewyn	brandy
dagga	Marijuana
dankbaar	thankful
Dankie	thank you
darem	really
dingus	things; also excited
doppie	little tot (of drink)
dop	tot
dring	slang for "drink"
Garn	go on
Gesondheid	good health
Het	Greetings
Hoit	Greetings
howkees	barrow boys – also a form of exclamation
jol	dance, party
jong	young man
juba	bloke, buddy, girl friend
mos	just (as in "just a little") but also used freely
ne	Isn't it? Not so?
Onder deze piesang boompie al op een eilandtje …	under this banana tree on an island
oomie	uncle
ou	old, old man
ouens	fellows
ou kerel	old person, old man
pikkie	child
pondok	shanty
pondokkie	diminutive of "shanty"
rommel	wandering around, messing about
shel	moody
skel	scold
skollies	hooligans
soldat	soldier
waar's dies dagga	where's this dagga (marijuana)

171

The Author

Alex La Guma, who lives with his family near Cape Town, is at present under house-arrest for his activities against South Africa's race laws. Prior to his confinement to his home for five years by the authorities, he was arrested and tried for treason with a large number of other South Africans, and acquitted after a four-year trial. During the 1960 state of emergency in South Africa, he was imprisoned for five months, and in 1961, detained for twelve days and charged with organising a general strike. Thereafter he was prohibited from attending any gatherings in the Republic of South Africa, ordered to resign from political organisations and debarred from joining any trade union. He was placed under house arrest last year.

According to South African political laws, none of Alex La Guma's writings may be published or distributed in the Republic. Many of his stories have been published in other parts of Africa, U.S.A., Germany, Sweden and South America.

Of his first novel, "A Walk In The Night", published in Nigeria, the critics said:

"He has his finger on the pulse of the people . . . one of the most significant contributions to South African literature." *New Age,* Cape Town.

"A most interesting work . . . too hot to hold in South Africa." *Cape Times,* Cape Town.

"This intense story, written with startling realism . . .

evoked many bravos from writers. . . ." Kampala
Writers Conference, Uganda.

"The master hand of a writer... powerful realism...."
S. A. Information and Analysis.

"Among the most beautiful literary pieces to have
come out of South Africa for a long time." Ezekiel
Mphahlele, *"Writers of Africa," Fighting Talk*, South
Africa.

"Very brilliantly done." *Nigeria Magazine.*

"It has achieved what several novels by African
writers, three to four times its length are still merely
groping towards." Wole Soyinka, *Lagos Post.*

"One of the most exciting books to come out of South
Africa." *Oklahoma University Press.*

SEVEN SEAS BOOKS
Glinkastrasse 13–15 · Berlin W 8

FICTION

Gina Berriault	THE DESCENT*
Millen Brand	SOME LOVE, SOME HUNGER
Mena Calthorpe	THE DYEHOUSE
Haakon Chevalier	THE MAN WHO WOULD BE GOD
Jack Cope	THE FAIR HOUSE
Margot Heinemann	THE ADVENTURERS
Xavier Herbert	SEVEN EMUS
Dorothy Hewett	BOBBIN UP
Stefan Heym	THE CRUSADERS (2 vol.)
Stefan Heym	THE GLASENAPP CASE
Lars Lawrence	MORNING NOON AND NIGHT**
Lars Lawrence	OUT OF THE DUST**
Farley Mowat	PEOPLE OF THE DEER***
Abraham Polonsky	A SEASON OF FEAR*
Alexander Saxton	THE GREAT MIDLAND
Alexander Saxton	BRIGHT WEB IN THE DARKNESS*
F. B. Vickers	THE MIRAGE

NONFICTION

Wilfred Burchett	COME OVER THE MAN
W. E. B. Du Bois	AN ABC OF COLOR
Norman Freehill	CHINA – ALL ABOUT IT!
Ezekiel Mphahlele	DOWN SECOND AVENUE
Mark Twain	KING LEOPOLD'S SOLILOQUY
Alan Winnington	SLAVES OF THE COOL MOUNTAINS

SHORT STORY COLLECTIONS

Ed. Gertrude Gelbin	FOLLOWING THE SUN
Walter Kaufmann	THE CURSE OF MARALINGA
Richard Rive	AFRICAN SONGS
John Reed	ADVENTURES OF A YOUNG MAN

---

* Not for sale U.S.A. or Canada
** Not for sale U.S.A. or Great Britain
*** Not for sale Canada

THE CLASSICS

George Eliot	SILAS MARNER
Ed. Gertrude Gelbin	SONG TO GENERATIONS
Ed. Kay Pankey	SPOOKS IN YOUR CUPBOARD
Ed. Hans Petersen	SEA TALES OF THE SEVEN SEAS
Walt Whitman	POETRY AND PROSE

ENGLISH TRANSLATIONS FROM THE GERMAN

Willi Bredel	THE DEATH OF GENERAL MOREAU
Jurij Brězan	THE FALLOW YEARS
Stephan Hermlin	CITY ON A HILL
Translated by	IMMORTAL LIEDER –
E. Louise Mally	800 Years of German Poetry
Anna Seghers	TWO NOVELLAS
Short Stories	A PAIR OF MITTENS
Short Stories	OLD LAND, NEW PEOPLE
Short Stories	THEY LIVED TO SEE IT
Bodo Uhse	LT. BERTRAM
F. C. Weiskopf	THE FIRING SQUAD
Arnold Zweig	A BIT OF BLOOD

A DOUBLE-HEADER FOR FREEDOM!

| BLACK THUNDER | by Arna Bontemps |
| AND WHY NOT EVERY MAN? | ed. Herbert Aptheker |

OTHER NEW TITLES JUST OFF THE PRESSES

THE EYES OF REASON	by Stefan Heym
THE FABULOUS AMERICAN	ed. Hilda Lass
A Benjamin Franklin Almanac	
MY MASTER COLUMBUS	by Cedric Belfrage
AUSTRALIANS HAVE	ed. Gertrude Gelbin
A WORD FOR IT	
A MORNING TO REMEMBER	by Herbert Smith
AND A THREEFOLD CORD	by Alex La Guma

A SEVEN SEAS SPECIAL!

| IT WILL BE A LOVELY DAY | HEINRICH HEINE |
| Selections from his Prose Works | |

Briefly,
ABOUT THE AUTHOR

Alex La Guma who wrote "And A Three-fold Cord", has been a fighter for his people and against apartheid since he was grown enough to think. In October, 1963, as the result of his fearless struggles, he and his wife, Blanche, were arrested under a "No trial" detention law. At the time of their arrest, they were under twenty-four hours a day house arrest in the Coloured area of Cape Town. Taken from their two small sons, they were thrown into prison. Prior to his arrest, Mr. La Guma had finished a splendid first novel, "A Walk In The Night", and while under house arrest he wrote the current novel, "And A Three-fold Cord". An excellent biography of the author is to be found in the Foreword to the current volume. This was especially written for the Seven Seas Books edition by Brian Bunting, poet and essayist, and a leader in the anti-apartheid struggle.